OUR TOUCHDOWN SCRIPT

A SCALA TALENT AND
SPORTS MANAGEMENT NOVEL

NICOLE VIDAL

COPYRIGHT

Published by: Jasper Media, LLC

Cover design by Ashlee Nassar of Designs with Sass
Cover photo by Roman Seliutin
Developmental Edit by Katherine McIntyre of Hot Tree Editing
Final Edit by Sharron McKenzie of Hot Tree Editing

ISBN 978-1-961365-73-5

TABLE OF CONTENTS

KEEP IN TOUCH WITH NV

Facebook (http://fb.me/NicoleVidalAuthor)

Instagram (http://instagram.com/nicolevidal_author)

Amazon (https://www.amazon.com/Nicole-Vidal/e/B082DJHPXP?ref_=dbs_p_ebk_r00_abau_000000)

My website (www.nicolevidal.com)

Pinterest (http://pinterest.com/NicoleVidal_Author)

Goodreads (https://www.goodreads.com/author/show/19827329.Nicole_Vidal)

CHAPTER ONE

KELLAN

FEBRUARY 2026

The Scala offices are modern and well-appointed. Last season, my teammate Jordan Devereaux was traded to Atlanta. At his farewell party, I scored a meeting with Valencia Halden. She's a powerhouse agent who is sought after for her negotiation skills. I signed with her at the initial consultation. Today we're working on my finer details of my contract. Well, what I'm seeking at least. I'm an unrestricted free agent, which means I have completed four or more accrued seasons. I can sign with any club with no draft-choice compensation owed to my current team. I began my career in Seattle and then was traded to DC.

Truth is, I don't want to leave DC. More accurately, I don't want to leave my home. I live modestly. My choices were intentional. The spacious home is decidedly too large for only me. Maybe someday, it won't be. I've been in one place for the last six years. However, the ownership has made moves that have decimated our roster, including losing Jordan, who is the best wideout in the game along with a few key draft picks. For Atlanta, the trade was absolutely worth it. The remaining rostered players won't be able to compete without him and the others who left or were traded.

"Good morning. How can I help you?" a good-looking man in a tailored suit asks. I'm secure enough in my masculinity to admit another guy is up to par. To be honest, he seems familiar.

"Kellan Oaks. I have an appointment with Miss Halden."

"Nice to see you again. Micah has nothing but great things to say about you and your work ethic."

I wrack my brain trying to recall his name. He's married to Pollin. It's the same as a cookie brand. "You as well, Tate."

"Follow me. Miss Halden is finishing a call. She'll meet you in the conference room."

"Thank you."

"Would you like a beverage or snack?"

The customer service here is top-notch. "A bottled water would be great."

Tate ushers me into a small space with a rectangular table facing out to the rear of the building. The floor-to-ceiling windows boast a distant view of the city. He returns with the beverage and takes his leave.

About ten minutes later, my agent breezes into the room. "I'm sorry for my tardiness." If I wasn't friendly with her fiancé and hung up on one woman, I would consider chasing her. Valencia was a model before attending law school and becoming a sports agent. She's hot as hell. Her blonde hair, blue eyes, and legs for days are precisely my type.

"No problem." I sit across from her.

"How is your mom feeling?" she asks.

I'm the youngest of five and was a surprise addition to the family. My mother fell and broke her hip soon before our first meeting. "Much better. She has nearly regained complete mobility." I'm not surprised. Nellie Oaks is a force. My mother was determined to be fully capable of attending my home games without the assistance of a walker or cane. My siblings have built families of their own and are scattered along the East Coast. DC is a convenient middle ground for her to live… me too. I have ten nieces and nephews ranging from a high school senior down to a toddler. A niggle deep in my chest resurfaces. I want a family, but fatherhood hasn't worked out for me yet.

"Wonderful to hear. Let's move on to what you're looking for."

I sink deeper into the chair. "I'm not foolish. This contract needs to be heavy with guaranteed money. I have only a few solid years left to play this game."

"You're healthy," she states.

"I am, but I'm also realistic. The strain lasts longer following game day. Instead of feeling 100% on Monday, now it's more like Wednesday."

She nods and makes a few notes.

I continue. "I want to stay with DC. However, the roster is thin, and we won't likely make the playoffs unless the front office shakes things up this offseason."

Valencia tilts her head. "What is more important to you? Remaining in or winning?"

I have a ring. Championships are the metric by which nearly all careers are measured. I'll never reach Tom Brady heights of seven wins in the big game. Perhaps I have an outside chance for three rings like Travis Kelce. Old-timers, namely Marv Fleming and Randy Grossman, both tight ends, are tied with four rings apiece. "Honestly, both. It's unrealistic though. If I had to rank the two, I want another ring before I retire."

Valencia scribbles a list of teams on the paper in front of her: Atlanta, Los Angeles, Dallas, and DC. She turns the paper in my direction. "I can work these locations. Aside from guaranteed money, what are your requirements?"

My current team is there as a placeholder and nothing more. Leaving will give me the best shot I have to win again. My agent's list made it crystal clear.

"I don't have a dollar figure in mind. I've been smart and invested well. I'm ranked in the top five tight ends in the league in most categories. The most important are yards after catch and touchdowns. I lead those."

"I'm aware. Nothing else?"

I shake my head.

"No business concerns?"

"No, my location doesn't impact my other endeavors." I own a few car washes. I'm also a silent partner in a highly successful bistro in the capitol city.

"Got it." She wrinkles her nose as if her next question will be invasive. "Relationship concerns?" she asks.

My stomach bottoms out. An image of Demi flashes in my mind. “We aren’t together right now.” The staff is keenly aware of my on-again, off-again relationship as my ex is a Scala client as well.

“I’m sorry.”

Me too. I hoped we would’ve figured our shit out. Unfortunately, we haven’t despite my desire to do exactly that. She’s the one for me, but we can’t get on the same page.

Our history is as twisty as a roller coaster. We met twelve years ago. I was attending a premiere for a movie in New York City. The film included a high school football team. I was one of the players. A teammate of mine stumbled upon a request for extras in the film. We weren’t even credited. After the viewing, there was a reception at a nearby hotel. I’ve made great strides handling press and large crowds of people since the beginning of my career. Back then, I kept to myself. I slipped out of the party after greeting the necessary people and rode the elevator to the roof.

When I rounded the corner, a tall woman in a sequined dress was gazing out at the city lights.

I approached wide to the right so I wouldn’t startle her. “Do you mind if I hang out over here?”

She turned in my direction. She was stunning. Still is to this day with captivating blue eyes and flawless skin. “Of course.”

“Running away from the party?”

She moved closer to me. “Perhaps. You?”

I'm not sure what to make of her narrowing the space between us. "Not a fan of tons of people in one place."

"Same except… never mind, it doesn't matter. The view up here is spectacular. Isn't it?"

"Yes." I wasn't looking at the cityscape anymore. I was staring unabashedly at her. I couldn't pry my eyes away. Forces beyond my control were drawing me into her orbit. I refused to fight it. I took a step closer.

"The city lights are out there." She hitched her thumb out over the ledge.

I smiled at her. "I know. You aren't."

Her shoulders dropped, and she relaxed a bit. "Why are you hiding up here?"

"Needed some space is all. Stealing away from the event was worth it to meet you." We were about a foot apart at this point. I'd never met a woman as beautiful as her, not in real life anyway, until that night.

"You as well. Up here, I'm just me. Downstairs, I'm—besides I'm sure my handler will find me soon."

I remember wondering why she needed someone to watch her. When the door burst open and someone shouted, "Demi!" two facts came into immediate focus. First, she was the female lead of the premiere I watched. She was exceptional in the role. We never filmed at the same time. Second, she was too young for me to consider asking for her phone number or acting on the thoughts in my head.

Respecting women was ingrained in me from early on. Her age didn't stop the dirty thoughts from running through my mind though. My moral compass did prevent me from pursuing her. While I didn't know it at the time, Demi is at least five years younger than me.

"Kellan?" Valencia pulls me back to the present.

"My apologies. I'm currently focusing on finishing out my career ideally with another ring or two."

"I understand. While I wasn't in your position exactly regarding your relationship, right person, wrong time is a thing."

"Thank you. Please feel free to call if you have more questions."

She stands and extends her hand to me. "I'll be in touch."

I nod and exit the room before returning to my vehicle. My truck is a few years old and inconspicuous. Unlike other people in the league, I don't collect expensive stuff. The drive is only sixty miles, but the traffic in this area is off-the-charts insane. I pull into my garage two hours later.

I keep with my normal routine as much as possible in the offseason. My afternoon recovery session is long but worth it. Despite an overwhelming desire to forget Demi, Valencia's question about my relationships pulled her front and center. It doesn't help that the news channel on one of my gym screens flashes her name as an Oscar nominee for best actress in a drama.

Is my pining appropriate? The woman is one of the hottest people on the planet. Why not? She's an adult. Now we're exes but still friends. The issues weren't solely in our relationship. Our downfall was her parents even after she became an adult and our inability to be in the same place together for more than a few months at a time. I scroll through my sent texts list. We haven't spoken in a few months, yet our text thread going back to the night we met is among the few I keep active.

Me: Congratulations.

I don't expect a quick response. For all I know, she could be in a foreign country right now. This nomination is her first as a lead actress but second overall. Despite the space between us both literal and figurative, I'm proud of her. I doubt a second chance or fourth… is in the cards. Reopening communication is as good a start as any since she broke my heart when she walked away from us.

CHAPTER TWO

DEMI

"Have a good evening, Miss Goldberg," my driver states after wheeling my luggage to my front door.

"Jimmy, we've talked about this. Please, it's Demi. Say hello to Sasha, Emily, and Jack for me."

"I will." He waits for me to open the front door of my house. The space is huge. However, it met my other needs including privacy, acreage, and the stunning views of Point Dume. The hiking trails and lush landscaping are the perfect jaw-dropping escape for me.

It's been years, but the memory of my mom's dirty house still flashes in my mind when I return from a shoot. Her holey clothing and worn shoes, unkempt hair and lack of showering, and overall demeanor were symptoms I missed at my young age. The money I sent to run the household wasn't being used for its intended purpose. My mother was an addict. It's the main reason my father abandoned us. He left me to help her when I was too young to do it.

She has never nor will ever step foot in this home. I'm not difficult. My profession allows me to pay for the things I require. A clean home and stocked fridge are a must. Carol is a godsend and makes sure everything is ready when I finish a film. She has been my housekeeper since I bought this place about seven years ago. Carol cleans and makes sure I have food both prepared and ingredients for meals. I'm not a great cook, but I won't starve.

My last film was set in Italy. The country is gorgeous. The food is to die for when I wasn't on set. I only had two opportunities to explore. Otherwise, it wasn't home. I'm a creature of habit. Without a second thought, I walk to the laundry room and start a load of clothes. I have more outfits, but domestic tasks are soothing to me.

With a bottled water and a bowl of fruit, I wander outside to my patio and take a seat. The fresh air and stunning sunset settle me. While unusual for me, I shut off my phone earlier today. Award season is beginning.

Over the course of my career, I've been blessed with exceptional roles and directors. My film *The Woman in Black* from last year is short-listed for an Oscar. It was the third time I worked with Ellis Barnett. His screenplay and direction were impeccable. I'm not one to boast, but my performance of his nuanced and pitch-perfect words was monumental. I'm afraid to want the nomination let alone the award itself. I've been chosen for an Oscar in a supporting role before. I was young, naïve, and didn't win.

After a deep cleansing breath, I power on my phone. Numerous notifications chime. One stands out. Kellan has a personalized sound for his messages. Always has. When we were younger, I knew to find a private place to read or listen. Back then, his name was disguised, if you will. Now, a select handful of people have my personal number. Everyone else goes through my agent. Kellan and I have been on-again, off-again for years. We went through a myriad of ups and downs together but could never make it work long term. Most of our issues were certainly from my parents.

Not accurate. I refused to let him give up his career despite his offer. I loved him. If I'm being honest with myself, I still do. I swallow hard and open my text messages.

Kellan: Congratulations.

I don't bother looking at the actual announcement. Kellan wouldn't reach out to me for a team award. He would for a personal one though.

Me: Thank you. Where in the world are you?

Kellan: Home. You?

Surprisingly, he answers almost immediately given the time difference. It's nearly ten p.m. in Great Falls, Virginia.

Those four letters punch me in the gut. That was our main issue. We could never find a place to call home together. With our crazy schedules, we were apart more often than not.

Me: Home as well. I live in Malibu.

Instead of typing his answer, a video chat request pops on my screen.

I may be a sought-after, newly minted two-time Oscar nominee, but I accept the invitation without hesitation. Kellan has seen me first thing in the morning with makeup staining my face and dressed in couture gowns for premieres.

"Hi, Dolce." He chose it because the dress I was wearing when we first met was designed by Dolce & Gabbana. The word also translates to "sweet" in Italian. I used the name Knockout for him because at that time, he was the hottest guy I'd ever seen. Also, I didn't want anyone who had access to my phone to connect Kellan and the phone number.

I grin at his endearment for me. He didn't use it the last time we saw each other. Perhaps we were too busy fucking on every imaginable surface for nostalgia. In my heart, I know that isn't true. He was still angry and hurt. Now, he seems to have softened a bit. "It's nice to see your face."

"You too."

We stare at each other in silence for what seems like a year but totals at least a minute. He looks fantastic. Kellan hasn't aged a bit aside from adding about twenty pounds of lean muscle. He smiles, and my heart clenches when his dimple hollows out. It is one of my favorite attributes of his.

"Did you take your vacation yet?"

We aren't jumping into the deep end of conversation immediately. The last time we broke up five years ago was difficult. After that, we had an off-season booty call after my agent's wedding that lasted a few months. Our texts and chats have been few and far between as well as short on details and depth.

"No. I wanted to decompress at home after the horrible end of my season first."

"Your record wasn't your fault. The team can't expect to win after trading away the best players on the roster."

He smirks at me. "Checking up on me?"

"Never stopped. We may not be able to find a home base or enough time to grow together as a couple, but everything else in our relationship worked. Right?" My gut churns with conflicting emotions.

The only sacrifice we haven't made for each other is our careers. We've held strong during tough times like when Kellan was injured during training camp in his third season. He was there when my mother…. No matter what, when life was hard, Kellan and I were present for each other.

He gazes toward the ceiling and gathers his thoughts. It looks like he's in his bedroom judging from the pillows behind him. Silence echoes along the phone line from coast to coast.

"Kellan?" When he doesn't answer, I whisper, "I'm sorry." Our breakups, if you will, were generally mutual. The last and most difficult was my choice.

He exhales slowly and meets my gaze. "No apology necessary. You aren't wrong. When we are together in the same place, things are amazing. When our careers and locations clash, it sucks."

I couldn't have said it better myself.

He adds, "Our breakup seems to be working out for you. A second Oscar nomination is huge."

"That film was a heart-wrenching role but worth it."

"You were phenomenal."

"Checking up on me?" I echo his question from earlier.

"Never stopped."

My throat tightens when the gravity of my choice to end trying to be together settles in. I couldn't let him give up on his dream for me. I love the fact he was willing to do it, but I felt like he would regret his decision later in our life.

"Maybe we should move on?" I suggest. Nothing has changed. I'm uber-busy with filming, and he's a successful professional football player.

"To what?" he asks.

We spent hours upon hours hashing out the pros and cons of long distance and lengthy periods of time apart. Nothing has changed. "Are you staying in DC?"

He drags his hand down his face. "Probably not. Valencia knows her stuff. My team has no chance to make the playoffs. She created a list of teams that have a need for my unique skill set."

"Cap room too?"

He laughs heartily. "Yeah."

"Willing to share where?" I ask. A sliver of hope he could be closer to me, despite our current friends-only status, blooms in my heart. We're more than that. We know every inch of each other from scars to birthmarks and emotional pitfalls.

"Atlanta, Los Angeles, and Dallas. Val left DC on the list, but the inclusion was for me. The front office would be wise to trade me for younger players."

A small part of me cheers. He could be closer for two of the teams. Does his location change anything between us? I would love nothing more. Will it? Probably not. "All three give you a great chance to win another ring, especially Atlanta with Jordan."

His eyes widen, and he shakes his head.

"What?" I ask, wondering the cause of his concern.

"That was pretty much what I said to Val."

A laugh bubbles from my belly.

"One of my favorite sounds."

Every time he's nice to me makes me rethink if my decision was right. My gut said he would regret choosing me. Fun and light calls like this give me pause. Did I give up the best man for me based on some sense of misplaced reverse chivalry?

"Thank you."

"Welcome."

"When will you know where you're going to end up?"

He shrugs. "Within a month or so. Why?"

"If the West Coast calls, perhaps we could share a meal?" Fear of rejection zips through me. I hurt him when I refused to let him retire. He told me as much.

A gorgeous smile graces his face, masking a slight hesitance, in my opinion. "That sounds great. It was nice talking to you. We should do it more."

"Yes. Good night, Kellan." I close my mouth to let my brain catch up before "I love you" pops out.

"Sweet dreams, Dolce."

I end the call and stare at the dark sky over Point Dume. Would we be able to make us work if he were traded to Los Angeles? My filming schedule this year isn't as nuts as the last three. Plus, only one is outside of my home state. Ironically, the location is in Maryland.

I squash the butterflies in my heart, mind, and belly. He said talking, not marriage. He's my person, and I look forward to sharing more with him again.

CHAPTER THREE

KELLAN

Rekindling my relationship with Demi on paper would be perfection. As she said, the issue was time together and building a home. We broke up because she refused to allow me to retire. I know how that sounds. Refused. I was willing to give up my career and follow her around to gain face time and proximity.

Instead of accepting my offer, Demi walked away from me. Devastation would be an apt description of my response. My life was rough for a while. I found myself dialing her number and hanging up. Unhealthy would be another way to explain the same.

My college roommate yanked me out of my funk. Darius Mosby pounded on my door three mornings after she left. He kept showing up until I was acting semi-normal again. He's a standup guy and great friend. He played linebacker in college. Darius was drafted in the later rounds but didn't make a fifty-three-man roster. He shifted to selling luxury real estate for athletes and celebrities. Darius married his college sweetheart, and they have three sons. Before I leave for the facility today, I send him a text.

Me: Hey, bro! Can you talk?

Darius: I'll call you in ten.

After driving to the stadium, I grab my gym bag and step out of my truck. My off-season routine includes a six-mile hike each morning. Normally, I would be outdoors, but today I'm using the simulator at the facility. Plus, I will be left alone. The team gym is a ghost town this early.

I start the system and select my path. As soon as I get moving, my phone rings.

I answer through my headphones. "What's up?"

Darius laughs. "Morning to you too."

The pad incline increases, and I push on. "How are Roni and the boys?"

"She's kicking butt and taking names as the CFO of her company. My sons are amazing, but they never sit still for longer than a minute."

I grin. "Maybe you're secretly wishing for a daughter now."

"No way. One woman is all I can handle. How are things with you?"

Darius doesn't begrudge me my success in the sport we both love. "I'm working the free agent market."

I imagine my friend shaking his head. "You don't need me to assess your options. How is Demi?"

My heart sinks. Do I only call him when it's about Demi? "How do you know?"

"I'm your brother from another mother. She's the only person on the planet who will make you reach out for advice from an old married guy."

I chuckle again and continue along the path on the screen. "We aren't old. You are one of a few happily married guys I know."

Darius understands both the football and non-football parts of life.

"Where are your options?"

I share the same information Val gave me with him while I continue walking.

"Did you look at their current rosters?" he asked.

"I have, but you and I both know, the players could be drastically different by the season opener in six months." Atlanta is looking for a tight end and a wideout. Los Angeles needs those positions plus a safety. Dallas is the same plus a solid veteran quarterback. The current player holding the spot had a horrid season last year.

"True, but you have to prioritize what you want. Is it her or rings?"

"Both." *Always have.* "I was willing to give up everything for her before. I may be getting a little bit ahead of myself. She invited me to dinner when I go to the West Coast for my interview."

"She's not working at the moment?"

"I opened the conversation with congratulatory wishes. We talked for a bit. I only know she's home now." Perhaps I should've asked. I'm willing to jump headlong into a relationship with her again without all the details. Foolish, I'm aware.

"I know she's your better half. So does Demi. The two of you need an honest, hard-core, no-holds-barred conversation if you start over. You both need to be all in, or it won't work." Darius sums up the twisty thoughts in my head in a few succinct sentences.

Demi is the love of my life. I want another shot to make it work. "You're saying start slow then."

"Bro. I was there to pick up the pieces of your shattered heart. I know she's the only woman who ever made you feel worthy. Be sure if you try again. I don't believe you can recover a second time."

Not sure I did from the first time. I've spent the last five years going on first date after first date. The women were CEOs and business owners and even a rock singer. They were accomplished like Demi in different industries. I never found anything remotely close to what I had with Demi from only phone calls and texts.

"I hear you. I've been drawn to her since the moment we met. I can't shake her. Honestly, I don't want to. I tried and failed to move on."

"I had a front row seat. You deserve to be happy. You've always wanted to create a home and fill it with kids. You failed there last time."

He isn't wrong. We were never in the same place for more than a few months. Our time together was too short to continue to build what we started all those years ago when we were young and naïve about the real world.

"Thanks, man. I appreciate the talk."

"You're welcome. I expect a visit and tickets if you land in Atlanta."

I grin. "Deal. I'll fly you and the fam out to a game wherever I suit up in the fall." The call ends, and I continue my walk. The sun hasn't risen yet for her. I imagine her in a king-size bed curled up in a fetal position near one of the corners.

The system alerts me to the last quarter of my program, and the walking pad slows significantly. I finish up, shower, and return to my truck.

Once seated, I dial my agent.

"Good morning, Scala Talent. How may I direct your call?"

"Valencia Halden please. This is Kellan Oaks."

"Nice to hear from you. Maybe I can help you? She's in a meeting already this morning."

"Tate?"

"The one and only."

"I want to send flowers to Miss Goldberg for her nomination. Can you provide the address to Flowers Galore in Los Angeles?"

"I'd be happy to."

"Thank you. Please say hello to Micah for me." Micah is Tate's husband and my DC teammate.

"Will do. Have a nice day, Mr. Oaks."

I shake my head. I don't know how many times I've requested he use my first name.

I ask Google for the number. My phone instantly pulls the information from my contacts. I never deleted anything pertaining to our relationship, including her favorite flower shop. After pulling out of the lot, I place an order with instructions Scala Talent will provide the address.

When I arrive home, I grab some food and tackle some work in my office. I monitor my businesses at least every other day. A few hours later, worried I'm about to overstep, I call Demi.

"Hey there!" she answers immediately.

"Hi. Is it too early?"

She guffaws. In my head I see her waving her hand as if to indicate the call is no big deal. “Not at all. Jet lag didn’t hit me this time. How was your workout?”

I would frown, but she knows my routine is unlikely to change. “It was light and easy. Then I caught up on my businesses. You?”

“Still chillin’ with my morning coffee.”

“Have you decreased your consumption?”

Demi laughs heartily. “Not at all. Have you come over to the dark side yet?”

“Perhaps.” When we broke up, I restricted myself to only one cup of coffee a day.

“Do tell,” she urges.

I laugh. “I may have eased up a bit and enjoy more servings of joe every now and then.”

“Well, well, well. Good for you.”

“How’s it going there?” I ask. The last time she was nominated, we were together. The calls, flowers, and gifts were incessant. My flowers will be different from the others though. I also know Demi will donate the blooms from anyone other than her agent, Ellis Barnett, and me.

“I sent a truckload of flowers to the hospital before you called.”

“Did you keep any of the unconventional gifts?”

“Sadly, there weren’t any this time. The framed movie ticket you made me for my first nomination is the best unconventional gift I’ve ever received.”

We were off-again when her first film debuted in the theaters but on-again when it was award season. I saw the movie on opening day. I framed my ticket and gave it to her. I have a stub for each of her films. As far as I'm aware, she doesn't know I attend every project. Nearly all are from opening weekend except for one. We were playing in Mexico, and I couldn't pull it off.

"You never know." I stand and walk down the hall to my office. I open her drawer and locate the ticket for this nominated film. *Yes, she has a drawer in my home she's never been to.* I put it in an envelope and order another frame to match the previous design. If I'm lucky, I can bring it to her when I visit LA.

CHAPTER FOUR

DEMI

"I suppose there is still time for an unconventional gift to arrive." I have known Kellan more than half of my life. He is the only person who put me first. I threw that back in his face when I broke up with him. Shaking my head, I move onto a different topic. "How is Mama?"

He sighs heavily.

"Did I miss something?" Before I overthink, I switch to a video call.

His gorgeous face fills my screen after he accepts. "She fell in her front yard last summer and broke her hip."

I gasp and cover my mouth. "Oh, Kellan. I'm sorry." *Why didn't you call?* is on the tip of my tongue. Not blurting it out is the miracle of all miracles. Even when we were off, we showed up for each other.

"Thanks. She's a determined lady. Mama had a goal of walking without assistance to the last home game."

I nod. "I'm sure she was cheering in the family section." My stomach rolls. I pushed him and his supportive family away. The Oaks treated me better than my own.

"You know it."

A small laugh bubbles up. "And your siblings? What is the niece and nephew count these days?"

Kellan shares details about his family, including his ten nieces and nephews. “Marcus will be attending Bama in the fall.”

“Does he play a sport or is he a brainiac like his father, Aidan?”

Kellan tilts his head in surprise. My relationship with his oldest brother was rocky at best. Rather than address the past, he replies, “Both, actually. Marcus is a long-distance runner and top of his class.”

“Good for him.”

“What about your dad?”

My shoulders fall, but I share nonetheless. “As you know, my entire life Steven Goldberg, was a drunk.” Early on adjustments were made to meet my call times and auditions. Was his addiction an issue? He claimed it wasn’t. Any need for a drink or five each day would strike me as a problem. “I haven’t spoken to him since I cut him off.”

“I’m sorry.”

I wave Kellan off. “It was for the best. He was living off me without a meaningful familial relationship.”

“Radio silence for the decade?”

“Pretty much. Yeah.” My doorbell chimes, and I walk to the door. “Hang on a sec, someone is here.”

“Expecting company?”

I drop my head. “No, it’s probably more gift baskets and flowers. Don’t get me wrong, I’m grateful but….”

“You want something personal,” he states succinctly.

"Exactly." I reach the door, open it, and greet the older man with a newsboy cap. He's cute. His outfit screams Sunday best.

"Good morning, I have a large delivery for Miss Goldberg. Well, it's a few orders," the older man states.

"Hello. Please bring them in. You can set them on the dining table."

"Of course." He retreats to the van and opens the door.

I would offer to assist him, but I'm confident the assistance would be waved off. He sets down a large gourmet basket and exits the arched wooden door. Four trips later, he places a floral arrangement containing every favorite bloom of mine. Without a doubt, the bouquet is from Kellan.

"All set?" I ask.

"Yes, Miss."

I tip him.

He acknowledges the gratuity. "If I may be so bold, your performance was superb in your nominated film."

"Thank you. Have a lovely day."

"You as well."

I latch the door behind him and lift the phone to look at Kellan again. "You remember?"

"You left an indelible mark on my heart and soul, Dolce."

A close my eyes tightly for a moment to quell the brewing tears. "I…."

"I may not have agreed with our breakup, but it doesn't change what we shared."

Does he still love me as much as I love him? The obstacles haven't changed. Right? I push the thoughts away for a later time and smell the bouquet. It includes peach roses, white orchids, silver eucalyptus, and fuchsia ranunculus. "I appreciate you more than I can adequately express in this moment."

He bites his lower lip and drops his head. The mannerism is one of his tells. He has tons to say but doesn't plan on sharing right now.

I need to respect his silent statement and move on. "Any news from Val?"

Relief washes over his face that I'm not going to press him about us. Communication, verbal and nonverbal, was never an issue for us. "I have a call scheduled with her later today."

"Cool. Do you have a preferred team?" My heart drops to my feet, and I prepare myself for him to say Atlanta.

He pauses long enough for me to retract the question.

"You don't have to share. I get it."

My front door swings open, and Carol steps inside. I wave and retreat to the patio where my now cold coffee rests on the side table.

"Can I be honest with you?" he mumbles.

Perhaps he's ready to share now. Quick change of heart if you ask me. "Please do."

His shoulders fall before he sits up straight again in the tufted leather chair. Behind him is a large window overlooking what I would guess is the front of his home. "When I met with Val, she asked me if you were a consideration for my new team. I told her we weren't together anymore. Now, I'm confused. We aren't dating again. Are we heading that way? Is that what your dinner invitation was? A second chance? Or is it fourth? I don't recall."

I take a deep breath and process his words. "Is another try a possibility?"

Silence rushes back and forth along miles from Malibu to Great Falls. Our gazes are locked. I see pain and possible redemption in his expressive eyes.

Swallowing hard, I continue, "Let's set aside the fact we live on opposite coasts. I hurt you. I own that. You admitted it to me yourself. I couldn't believe you wouldn't resent me later in our life if you chose me over football. Maybe I had no right. Perhaps I did. I love the fact you would've put me before the game and your lucrative contracts. Does this only work if you end up in LA, or are we reverting to visits between shoots and away games?"

Kellan drags his hand down his face. "I love you. I never stopped. Probably always will. I don't know if our fourth or whatever number chance is possible if I'm not in the same city as you. Could it be worth it? Yes. Would I be willing to discuss it more in person? Absolutely."

I'm speechless. I spent time daily since our last breakup wishing, hoping, and praying for understanding from Kellan. Turns out, all I had to do was ask for another chance. My heart pounds, and tears threaten.

The devastation of our last breakup was palpable and cut deeply into us both, despite me being the one who inflicted the pain. "Really?" Kellan is the love of my life. Him bestowing upon us a fifth try seems huge. Hell, I know it is.

"Yes, but Demi...," he pauses, to enhance his next words, "This chance is our last. If we can't figure us out, I need to move on completely."

I manage to nod. He's right. We can't always have each other at the back of our minds as a secondary option. To me, Kellan is the reason none of my other dates made it past two. The unyielding ache our breakup left behind was ever present. Also, I heard what he didn't say. Kellan desires a few children, and he's older than me by five years. He doesn't want to be retiree age at a middle school graduation. The idea is flawed because he won't be playing anymore, but I imagine he has other plans after his football career ends. I suppose it's a topic we need to discuss.

My doorbell chimes again, interrupting our heavy but promising conversation.

"I'll let you go. After I speak with Val, I'll call back with more details," he states.

"You don't have to. Carol will get the door."

"I do. I need to wrap my head around possibilities I buried deep in my heart."

I draw my lips into a tight line and reply, "I understand. Talk to you soon."

He ends the call, and I crumble to the floor, clutching my phone in my hand. One final opportunity to be with the man of my dreams. Despite my desire to have him call me his again, I wrote it off as impossible. The agony on his face when I refused to let him choose us gutted me like a victim in a slasher movie. A self-inflicted wound. Hope bubbles in my veins. Mentally, I rush through my schedule for the next two years and wonder how we can pull off a rekindled relationship when nothing has changed since we broke up. We're both working busy with high-profile careers but this time we have a desire to make us last forever. The bigger question is… would I let him retire for me if the option is on the table?

CHAPTER FIVE

KELLAN

Ending the call with Demi was the right choice. Every word I shared was true. The prospect of rekindling our relationship unsettles me. I never stopped wanting her in my life. Our circumstances are unique. Emotionally nothing has changed since the moment I met her on the rooftop but geography was always our main issue.

Checking the time, I change into running clothes and take off out my front door. Cardio was planned for today, not yet though. I suppose if Demi and I are going to give us a try, our schedules will need to adjust. The miles will help me sort out my thoughts.

Admitting my feelings out loud to her was bold. If I need to run, she likely crumpled to the ground after hanging up. The floor is Demi's thinking spot. Mine is the road or a treadmill.

The looming question is my landing spot. To be fair, if we want our relationship to thrive, we have to put in the work. Will our relationship be harder if the best place for me is Atlanta or Dallas? No question. Los Angeles would be ideal as far as decreasing extra travel.

I ponder more and realize… retirement is still an option for me. I'm physically able to play, and I want to win again, but do I desire a life with Demi more? Demi and another championship ring are the goals. Pulling off our relationship and another championship has proven impossible in the past.

More so, I want a family. Demi is well aware of this desire. She isn't opposed to having kids, but timing is key. Some of her roles require her to be sans baby bump.

The more I consider a final chance with Demi, frustration creeps in. I see three options.

First, I can play football in a city other than where Demi currently resides regardless of the contract itself. We would need to plan for at least the season and her filming schedule. Demi would have to be willing to relocate wherever I'm playing and travel to away games.

Second, I choose LA and live with Demi. It would decrease the travel for her to only away games and her filming locations.

The final option is retirement. My gut rumbles thinking about it now. I offered to leave the game before. I'm not ready to do it again. I understood her position. Truly, there's no way to know if I would've resented her later on. I don't think I would've harbored ill feelings, but it's impossible to be that self-aware years in advance.

The paths all hinge on one thing. Demi's schedule. I pause at the corner and glance at my watch. Crap! I'm three miles in, and it's only been nineteen minutes. I take a few deep breaths and set a slower pace before turning back toward home.

I have a small window of time to shower and change before my call with Val. With a post-run protein shake in hand, I open the video conference link from my office.

"Hello, Mr. Oaks," Tate greets me.

"How are you?"

"Great. Val is on her way, but she didn't want to keep you waiting."

I acknowledge him. "Much appreciated. How are you liking the DC area?" Tate's husband, Micah, joined the team last season.

"The proximity to the capital city is wonderful. I especially love the fine dining options. However, I'm keen on the location of our new home. It's peaceful, quiet, and private."

"I understand. My residence has the same features."

Val breezes into the room. Breathless, she plops down in the chair in front of Tate. "Sorry for my lateness."

"No problem. Bye, Tate."

He nods and leaves the screen.

"I'm late because I was working on another potential home for you."

Intriguing development. However, the teams on my list were the only playoff contenders in my mind. Unless Val learned more insider information. "Oh. Where?"

"Phoenix," she answers with a huge grin on her face.

I can't school my face fast enough.

She adds, "You look shocked. What were you expecting me to say?"

"Seattle."

Val tilts her head. “They called too, but—”

“No cap room.”

“Exactly,” she grins.

“Are the others out of the running or do I have another option?”

“Los Angeles and Dallas have both requested a visit as did Phoenix. I can schedule them if you want.” My heart drops when she doesn’t say Atlanta. That team is the best place to reach the big game again. Plus, I could line up with Jordan.

“I would appreciate if you handled the meetings. Can you schedule them in a row?”

My agent frowns. “Please elaborate.”

“I would like to end in LA. I plan to spend some time there to relax after the facility visits.”

Val acknowledges my words. Her facial expression fails to mask the interest in my vacation spot selection. She knows Demi lives in the City of Angels. Sharing the potential rekindling of my relationship doesn’t seem necessary. I’ll select the best fit when I have all the information, including if Demi and I are a couple.

She continues, “When is the soonest you can leave?”

“Tomorrow?”

“Very well. I’ll set things up. Either Tate or I will reach out with the details.”

“Perfect. Thanks, Val.” I end the call and pace aimlessly. Then, I sit on my back porch staring into the wooded area in the rear of my home.

Balancing all the options isn't going to be easy. Demi Grace Goldberg yearns for another shot at a relationship. I never wanted to break up. While I tried to move on, I've failed in epic fashion. The lack of tabloid photos or whispers of private dinners with other men would indicate she hasn't had any luck either with other men.

Should I invite her to these visits, or is that overkill? Only one person can talk me through this. I grab my phone and dial.

"Hey, sweetie," she answers on the first ring. Mama never fails to be there for her children.

"Have a few minutes?"

"Always. What's on your mind?"

I spend some time sharing my calls with Val and Demi, including the options for my team to perhaps spending the rest of my life with the woman I love.

"That's a heavy burden, Kellan." Her statement is to the point and honest.

"I know. Right now, I have a list of possibilities and numerous paths I could follow."

Mama is quiet for a few moments. The silence forces doubt to take residence in my chest. The tightness grows until she adds, "You need to decide what you want. I'm not a fool. Neither are you. Demi is the love of your life. The sacrifice to make your relationship work must be borne by both of you nearly equally."

In the past, most of the give was on me. I was willing to be flexible, but it wasn't enough. Honestly, it was difficult to maintain high-level play and our home. In the present, we both have means to travel as necessary. What does her filming schedule look like this year? Next year?

"I agree, Mama. Should I invite her to the team visits?"

In my mind, I see her pursing her lips and taking a moment to select her words carefully. That doesn't happen.

Her answer is quick and unwavering. "No. You need to check out the locations on your own. If you want to involve her in the selection process, the decision is up to you. Do the tours without photogs and questions about your relationships. It's no one's business but yours. Plus, is another chance definite?"

I never have, nor ever will harbor ill feelings toward Demi despite our turbulent relationship.

"Being a couple takes work for regular people. The two of you don't qualify. The money and fame don't make it easier. In fact, they do quite the opposite."

"Thanks, Mama. You never fail to have the right words to ease my concerns."

"You're welcome. I love you, son. I hope this time works out for the two of you."

"Me too. I'll send you my itinerary when I have it." Mama doesn't like any of her children to leave their home state without sharing the travel details with her. Even my nephews and nieces provide their whereabouts.

"Good luck, Kellan. Focus on you first, then add in another try with Demi."

I was seeking clarity by reaching out to my mom. Unfortunately, she didn't offer additional insight. I was on the fence about inviting Demi but leaning toward not. Mama's opinion solidified my position. I amble to my bedroom and pack for my trip. A renewed sense of giddiness courses through me over not only for checking out my potential teams but spending time with Demi to see if we can finally make an us work for the long term.

CHAPTER SIX

DEMI

I need a friendly, understanding ear. Kellan fills the role for me. Well, he usually does. I can't talk to him about him at least not yet.

Me: Are you home?

Stell: Yes. Need company?

Me: Please.

Stell: Be there in thirty.

I haul myself off the floor and pad to the kitchen.

Carol is pulling a baking dish out of the oven. Any meal she prepares, I'll eat.

"Smells delicious."

Carol dotes on me more since losing her son to cancer a few years ago. I understand her type of loss. I shake my head and refocus on now. My therapist would urge me to share my thoughts on my mother's death, but dwelling doesn't suit any purpose for my life today. She's gone. I can't change reality. Harboring anger won't do me any good. I did everything I could to help her handle her addictions. My father on the other hand....

"You're too skinny," she replies.

"I appreciate you, Carol."

"I know, sweetie. Any progress with Kellan?"

I frown and whip my gaze to hers.

She adds, "You don't talk to anyone except him and Estelle on that phone for more than ten minutes."

She's right. "Possibly. We're going to get together and discuss a potential us when he visits the team facility here."

"He's willing to try again?" I hired her soon after our last breakup. It was splashed all over the entertainment blogs and podcasts. She was also aware of our fling after Madeleine's wedding. I hid on set as the publicity died down. Despite it being my decision, our breakup crushed me. I spent nearly two weeks on set like a zombie. It took deep soul-searching and an epiphany of sorts to move on. Kellan would have retired and been miserable. I did the right thing in the long term. In the present, I'm devasted.

I sigh heavily. "He's agreed to discuss it with me in person, but Kellan did indicate this time would be our last chance."

"How do you feel?"

Elated mostly. "Mixed, I guess. I believe him. Kellan doesn't hedge or mince words, especially with me."

Carol rounds the Carrara island in my kitchen and throws her arms around me. After a few short moments, she pulls back and adds, "You better figure out how to manage this chance then. Right?"

I pull my lips into a tight line, knowing she's correct. "Yeah. Estelle is on her way." Estelle Gomes is my girl bestie. She's an exceptional vocalist and client of Madeleine's as well. The music world classifies her as a pop artist. However, she could sing the phone book, and it would be mesmerizing. Aside from Carol, she's my go-to for everything.

"I'll prepare two plates."

"Thanks." I don't need to worry about my appearance but decide to freshen up anyway. Ten minutes later with a smoother messy bun and clean running hoodie, I greet my bestie.

We hug for a long time. "I'm so excited to see you. It's been a few months."

Stell frowns. "More like eleven."

I purse my lips and think back. *Has it been that long?* Am I a crappy friend as well as girlfriend? Did I try when Kellan and I were together to carve out enough time for us? Answering those questions is going to take some thought and effort. I'll consider it more after I hang with my girl for a bit.

"Dang. Let's dish over Carol's meal."

We pass through the kitchen and carry our food to the living room. Curling my legs under me, I rest the plate on the arm and ask, "How have you been?"

Estelle smiles. "Not as good as you, professionally at least."

"Thanks. What happened?"

"My last album sales weren't as high as my team would like. They claim I'm too old for pop music and I should change genres."

I finish my bite of the casserole. "How do you feel about that?"

My friend shrugs and sets her fork down. “Singing is in my blood. I can’t go a day without it, but I’m scared to try a different genre of music.”

“Plenty of people before you have done it. Greats like Taylor Swift and Lady Gaga have been successful.”

She scoffs. “I’m not in the same category as those icons.”

I cover her hand with mine. “You are. I’m strongly suggesting before you pursue other avenues like hosting or coaching to lay down a few tracks of contemporary or country music.”

Estelle tilts her head as if pondering my words. “Really?”

Leaning forward, I set my plate on the tufted ottoman and hug her. “Your range is insane, but you don’t showcase it.”

Her face flushes with joy. “Love you, bestie.”

“Love you back.”

My friend shifts her legs and asks, “What’s been going on with you? Any guys I need to check out?”

“I wrapped filming last week, then awards season began.”

“Congrats.”

I shake my head. “You know I don’t act for awards. It’s an honor to be nominated. That’s the line, right? I’ll admit, I want to win this time. This film is my best work. Your flowers were insane by the way.”

She acknowledges my statement.

I continue, “To answer your other question, Kellan messaged me congratulations. Fast forward a few chats and we agreed to talk.”

Estelle jumps to her feet, drags me with her, and leads me in a dance around the living room. We crumple back onto the couch out of breath before she adds, "Girl! Don't screw this chance up!"

"Well, we will discuss it, but he did say it would be our last chance."

"Why did your on-again periods fail in the past?" my gorgeous friend asks.

Not enough time together mostly. "The cause I need to figure out and then how to fix it."

"Longevity in a relationship was not something I was blessed with. I'm willing to listen though." Estelle married her childhood sweetheart, Charlie. He tragically died in a car accident before their second anniversary. If I recall correctly, she's been alone for at least four years.

"Did you decide on an Oscar designer yet?"

I sigh. "No, but I'm sure a few will be clamoring to dress me. I would prefer to stick with Kelly. She's talented and knows when to take risks." Kelly Barnett is a couture fashion designer. We met on her first job as a costumer for one of Ellis's films. They are married and have two kids.

"Makes sense."

My phone chimes, and I know from the sound, it's Kellan. As much as I want to hear about his call, I continue my catchup chat with Estelle. Near three, she leaves for a dinner reservation with her family.

I scramble to check my messages. To be honest, I'm proud of myself for not doing the same while my friend was visiting.

Kellan: Reach out when you're free.

His tone doesn't sound ominous. Good. Val is one of the best agents in the world. Before I return his call, I parse through the flowers and gifts that arrived. I shift the flowers from Scala to the kitchen and then schedule a pickup for the rest. Early in my career, I brought flowers to nearby hospitals or nursing homes personally. Now, visits require security. Believe me, I'm grateful for my success. Sometimes I wish… kind gestures didn't require fanfare and bodyguards. I've tried to sneak in late in the evening or early in the morning, but the last two times, my appearance was leaked and caused issues with the paparazzi around the hospital.

I settle the butterflies in my stomach and return Kellan's call via video chat.

He answers quickly. "Hey!"

"How was your meeting?" I ask. Kellan looks freshly showered and is wearing different clothes than earlier today. Inwardly, I frown and attempt to figure out when he worked out. If it was before his call with Val, his extra running is on me. Why? I refocus on now and add an entry to my list of things to figure out.

"Promising. She set me up with three visits starting tomorrow."

"Any surprises?"

He drops his head. "Phoenix actually."

"They have cap room, but their offense is pretty barren."

Kellan laughs heartily. "My initial thoughts were similar. However, Val assured me they have a few roster moves in the works. I don't know who yet, but Val indicated a visit would be in my best interest."

I tug my lower lip between my teeth. “Which one backed out?”

“Atlanta.”

“I’m sorry. That team was your preferred spot.”

He opens his mouth to speak but pauses. “Why do you say that?”

“It gives you the best chance to win another ring.”

“True, but their salary offer won’t meet my requirements.”

I bite my tongue and refrain from asking the obvious question. His contract details will be widely publicized given his stature in the league. Money was never an issue for us. Even at the beginning, after I hired a financial planner, we split everything in half. If we succeed as a couple this time, will it be different? Probably, but the possibility seems so far in the future. Maybe after we talk in person, I’ll feel differently.

“When will you be here?” Angst wraps around me as I ask the question. We’re tiptoeing around our potential relationship at this point.

He reaches for a piece of paper on his kitchen island. “Thursday.”

I exhale sharply.

“Talk to me, Dolce.” His tone is soothing but also exudes his concern for me.

“It’s fine. We’ve waited this long. I can handle a few more days.”

“Are you sure?” he mumbles.

“Yeah. I want to chat with you about us face-to-face but still want to talk until you get here. Does that make any sense?”

He laughs. “I understand. Will you share your address?”

I frown deeply. "You sent me flowers. How, if you don't know where I live?"

"Tate," he answers quickly.

I drop him a pin. "Good luck, Kellan."

"Thanks." We end the call so he can finish packing for his visits.

Flopping onto my bed, I think back to the times we were together. Kellan did all the traveling. It made sense during the offseason for him to come to set. When I was filming during games, we never saw each other. *Crap!* The reason for our breakups was time, and our failures were completely on me.

From the moment we met, I had no doubt Kellan was my person. If this is our last chance, I will be a better partner and share the burden. I resolve to figure out my schedule and, when we know where he's going to play, determine who is traveling when and where. Seeing the areas of concern and small gaps of time to spend together is the only way to truly give this final chance my all.

CHAPTER SEVEN

KELLAN

FEBRUARY 2018

The guys' trip was fun and needed despite the fact I missed Demi fiercely.

"Dolce, I'm home."

Clad in leggings and one of my team sweatshirts, which is three sizes too large, she runs across the gleaming hardwood and leaps into my arms. We have been living together in Seattle as our schedules allow since the draft two years ago.

She peppers my face with kisses before greeting me. "Hi. How was your weekend?"

"Good. It was nice to hang out with my friends and not worry about anything to do with football. I love my job, but I don't want it to be everything I am."

She wrinkles her button nose. "So you want…."

"You and a family… eventually. Two kids at least. What's going on in your pretty head? Not news to you."

Demi smirks. "No, it isn't. We're going to have to be purposeful and work around the craziness of our life."

“If anyone can pull off forever, we can.” We’ve already cleared some hurdles in our relationship, especially the difference in our ages as well as hiding from the press and entertainment media. To be honest, her parents remain difficult to deal with. Mostly, Beatrice.

“As long as my mother stays in treatment.”

Beatrice Goldberg spiraled when Demi left. Both of her parents attempted to get her to return home after her audition. Instead, Demi paid a moving company to pack up her room and storage unit. Somewhere in the back of her mind, my woman knew keeping anything precious at home wasn’t wise. Her awards and memorabilia were stored in a temperature-controlled unit not far from their rental in New Jersey.

We didn’t realize then, but Beatrice’s actions were symptoms of major depression and alcoholism. When Demi wasn’t filming, her mother seemed normal. She would keep the house, cook meals, and spend time with Demi. When Demi would leave for filming, her routines would fall into poor patterns, and her symptoms worsened. Beatrice failed to clean, eat properly, and even lost her job on multiple occasions for not showing up.

She hid her issues for years. Demi’s father was aware of the condition. Rather than seeking solutions, he left them. That reason led others like his previous theft to support my position to keep Steven Goldberg at arm’s length. No one deserves to be disrespected or mistreated because of a medical condition.

“Aren’t you paying for it?” I ask.

"Yes. My money doesn't matter to my mother at all. She hates the fact I earn an excellent salary. She claims I act superior to her." Demi waves her hand as if her mother's actions and opinions don't bother her. I know the words hurt her deeply. "Either way, she must do the work."

"True," I reply. I hope the conviction in my answer is believable. I don't trust either of Demi's parents one bit. My feelings have more to do with my upbringing than anything else. My parents were solid. Since losing my dad, Mama is keeping herself busy tutoring students and visiting her kids and grandkids. Eventually, she will come to dote on mine and Demi's.

"What do you say to movie night?" my girl suggests.

"Sure. Let me change. Pick something funny. I'll be right back." I kiss her lightly, scoop up my bag, and disappear into the bedroom.

We have been keeping a low public profile as much as possible. We aren't seen together out and about frequently. While technically legal, our age gap is a talking point for reporters. So far, I haven't been on her arm at a premiere. They seem to conflict with away games. If attending was possible, I would still think twice to protect our privacy.

Our focus is us, not what the fans or anyone else thinks. Demi's parents are completely against our relationship. Mama loves Demi and is on board with any woman who makes me happy.

I throw my clothes into the hamper and stow the rest of my things. I change and return to the living room. While we both have plenty of money, our home is modest. I don't have a man cave unlike some of my teammates.

Someday, perhaps. Demi would definitely use the space as her career progresses.

I laugh as I settle onto the couch.

"What's funny?"

"I was thinking about the fact we don't have a media room for the movie superstar." *50 First Dates* starting Adam Sandler and Drew Barrymore is queued on the flat-screen.

She shakes her head. "I don't need one. Besides, if I learned anything from Ellis, Hollywood can be fickle. I may say the wrong thing or my next film could bomb. Then I'm no longer sought after, but a has-been."

"Never going to happen, sweetheart."

Demi leans over and kisses me deeply. "Thank you for believing in me."

"Of course. You should own your professional prowess though."

"Meaning?"

"You have eight feature films on your resume in the last four years. You've been nominated as a supporting actress for an Oscar. I don't even know how many Screen Actors Guild, Golden Globes, or Critic's Choice awards you've earned."

She turns to look at me more fully. "Not why I act."

"Enlighten me."

She sighs deeply. "At first when I was little, I worked mostly for my mom. I saw my father's lack of support both financially and emotionally."

"What was your first gig?"

"I thought I shared this already?"

I shrug. "Tell me again." I don't recall the specifics, if I'm honest. Supporting her career and living out my dream is what I want for us.

"My first job was for a holiday catalog for a clothing store. That led to a few more print jobs. The following year, I was in a commercial for the same company. By my eighth birthday, I was reading for roles on television series. I played the sick kid on a medical show, the birthday party guest on a drama series, and so many others."

"How did you land your first movie?"

Demi grins. "Happy accident. Serendipity."

I grab her and haul her into my arms. "Please share with me. I don't recall this."

"Oddly enough, I was with my dad. Looking back and knowing about my mom's depression, she asked him to take her place. Forcing Dad to chaperone was a cry for help. Steven Goldberg ignored it though. He huffed the entire day. I had a magazine ad shoot in the Big Apple. The location was double-booked for my last hour and the first hour for a movie. One of the frazzled producers mistook me for the young actress meant to play the daughter in the movie."

I laugh. "Perhaps you are exactly where you're meant to be."

"I agree. You know the rest."

With a shrug, I start the movie. Demi doesn't even make it halfway through. I'm not surprised. She doesn't sleep well at home when I'm away. I shut off the comedy and lift her into my arms. Once she's tucked in, I strip off my clothes and slide into bed behind her.

First thing the next morning, I reach over and find her side of the bed ice-cold. When I check the time, I notice it's nearly ten.

Demi is sitting on the patio staring at the water view near our home in Seattle when I leave the bedroom.

"Morning, sweetheart. Everything okay?"

She tilts her head, then drops it. "I guess. My mom checked herself out of the treatment facility last night because she's fixed."

I sit beside her, scoop her into my arms, and hold her. I murmur near the shell of her ear, "I'm sorry."

"Me too. I can't do anything else. I'm providing the means for her to get well. My mother doesn't want the help." The weight of her family is heavy on her shoulders. Demi's father doesn't care one bit about his ex-wife or whether she is getting the treatment she needs. He made his position abundantly clear when Demi took off to be with me. Steven Goldberg disowned his daughter when she fired him as her manager and refused to support him financially in perpetuity. Hurtful words were exchanged, and they haven't spoken since, although Demi has reached out.

"How can I help?"

She lifts her gaze to mine and mumbles, "You're my rock. I can't imagine doing life without you beside me. I love you. I'm glad you're mine."

I kiss the top of her head. "I love you. I've got you as long as you'll have me."

She nods and pushes to her feet. "Ready to pack?"

"Let's eat something first."

One thing about Demi is she's a basic cook. We know our roles in the house, and food is decidedly mine.

I prepare a hearty breakfast consisting of omelets with ham and veggies, a side of sourdough toast, along with a small yogurt as well.

Tomorrow we leave for her film shooting in London for three months. The ability to attend with her is amazing. It'll be my first time abroad and on set with Demi. I'm looking forward to exploring and watching her practice her craft for the silver screen.

Demi and I are making significant progress in our relationship. We started building a solid foundation of friendship first, and it has helped us thrive in the early days. I will give her everything she needs to succeed in Hollywood and beyond. The fact I also get to play the sport I love is a huge bonus.

CHAPTER EIGHT

DEMI

NOVEMBER 2018

I resist the urge to chuck my phone across the room. I'm not surprised. My mother has been struggling to cope with her illness and addiction to booze for years. In the last year, she's added various pills, including OxyContin. Clinical depression mixed with alcohol and pills makes symptoms worse, not better.

The doctor speaks again. "If you would like to see Beatrice one last time, you should come."

My lip trembles, but the tears don't fall. "Yes, I understand." I end the call and slowly sit on the chair beside me. I've received calls like this more than once. Each time I rushed to her side, and she pulled through. Dr. Phillipa is the first physician to urge a last visit. His tone and word choice hit me hard and seem genuine unlike the others.

My mother has been in and out of treatment facilities more times than I can count. I could determine the cost as I bankrolled each attempt, but it was never about the money. Only I held onto hope she would follow through.

I run through my schedule in my head. I have three days to spare before my next shoot. Instead of stewing, I hustle to our bedroom and hastily pack a bag while on speakerphone with Pemberton Airlines.

"I need a flight to New Jersey," I state.

"When, ma'am?"

"As soon as possible please?"

I hear the clicking of her keyboard. "I have a plane in Los Angeles. Please be at the private terminal outside Seattle in three hours. I will email details immediately."

"Thank you." I lift my bag, grab my purse, and slide into the buttery leather of my luxury SUV in the garage. As I pull away, I consider what Kellan is doing at his away game in Chicago. Although he's likely practicing, I call anyway.

He answers instantly. "Hey, Dolce."

"Are you done for the day?" I ask.

"No. Just a break. What's wrong?"

I exhale slowly and share the call for the umpteenth time. I sound like a broken record without a doubt.

"I'm sorry, sweetheart. Are you going?"

My heart hurts. I'm tired of the roller coaster she's put me on emotionally. "Yes. This feels different."

"I understand. If you need me to meet you, I will."

Warmth cascades through me. He never fails me. "This is likely a false alarm like the rest. I'll keep you updated. Love you."

"I love you."

When I reach the tristate area, visiting hours have ended. Could I push my way in? Probably. I've been here before. Wondering if my mother will pull through or not. This is no different from my perspective except for the doctor's words and tone. I check into a nearby hotel for the night and crash.

First thing the next morning, I grab some breakfast and take an Uber to the Beechwood Manor. Beatrice has been here at least four times in the last two years. I walk through the front door, and the stale smell of a closed unit and antiseptic smack me in the face.

"Could you direct me to Beatrice Goldberg's room, please?" My mother kept her last name. It's ironic. She hates her ex-husband. It is, however, a link to me, her Hollywood starlet daughter. A moniker she created and now loathes.

The young receptionist barely looks up. I guess that's good for me. I won't be recognized. "Room 1125." She lifts her arm and points. "Down the hall on your left."

"Thanks." I expected more safety protocols for a private mental health facility. I shake off my displeasure and walk down the long, soft, pink corridor. At least the walls aren't sterile white.

I reach the room and pause at the threshold. The most recent occasion I was summoned by her healthcare team, she was sitting up laughing when I arrived. Her providers called it a "miracle." More accurately, my mother wanted attention.

Stepping inside, I find a frail, skin-and-bones version of my mother lying in the bed. Her hair is matted to her head. When is the last time she bathed? I swallow down the urge to vomit.

"Mom?" I manage in a soft voice.

The woman in the bed rolls slowly toward the sound. "No. What are you doing here? Go away!" While forceful, her words are hoarse and raspy.

Before I say something I can't take back, I reply, "I'm sorry. What?"

The doctor breezes into the room. "Good. You came."

"Morning. What is going on here?" My question is directed at the physician.

The portly man gazes at my mother in the bed. "I'm sorry. She's the only chance you have."

I clear my throat and repeat myself. "What is going on?"

Now resting against the headboard, my mother answers. "I'm dying. I need a new liver. The only way I'm getting one is from a family member."

The audacity to insinuate I would be willing to donate part of mine is unfathomable. I frown. The doctor's call intimated my mother was ill. The small detail is only a portion of the story. She might live if I'm a match and give her part of my liver. My stomach pitches. *Hell no!*

Beatrice scowls and shouts at the doctor. "I told you not to call her. She won't help me. Let me die in peace."

Fury bubbles within me. "How dare you?" My stare is pinned on my mother. Her once-curvy frame is now gaunt and jaundiced.

Beatrice crosses her arms and stares at me defiantly. "I didn't reach out to you. He did and violated my wishes. I don't want you or your judgment here."

"Judgment? I have funded your treatment since you admitted it was necessary. Do you think this fancy facility is free? I've given time and money to find a plan and place for you to heal and grapple with your addiction and mental health. If I was judging you, wouldn't I have stopped paying and finding better options a long time ago?"

My mother shrugs. The noncommittal gesture makes me want to storm out the door and never come back. This is the first moment it becomes clear that my mother doesn't care about me, my support, or whether she lives or dies. The latter is a new development.

After a long pause, with a quivering lip, she adds, "Doesn't matter. I'm done fighting. No more shrinks, therapies, or drugs. Please leave. I don't want you here."

The doctor, who still looks sheepish from his decision to reach out to me without permission, attempts to intervene. "Bea, she's your only chance for a match. You don't qualify for the transplant list." In the recesses of his mind, he may also be worried about a lawsuit. The good news for both of us is he doesn't know who I am. I'm not one to announce my profession or accolades when I enter a room. My mother's doctor certainly hasn't put my name together. I'm grateful.

My mother shoots daggers from her eyes at him. "I don't care. I can choose to forego treatment. That is what I'm doing."

Despite my desire to retreat and never look back, I ask, "How invasive is this test? Does she have enough time for me to find out?"

"Don't answer her. I don't want anything from her!" she shouts.

I snap my blue eyes to her sunken face. "Else, you mean. Anything else."

Rather than reply, my mother scoots down on the bed and turns away from me. I shake my head, exit the room, and rush to the front lobby.

Dr. Phillipa follows closely on my heels. "Please reconsider," he calls from behind me.

I stop only to make sure he hears me. "No reason to. She doesn't want to know if I can help her more by giving her a piece of my liver. Honestly, I would rather not know if I'm a match. This is her choice."

He drops his head. Acknowledging my mother's position and mine is a hard pill for him to swallow.

"How long does she have? I would appreciate the truth this time."

The physician, whose last-ditch effort failed in spectacular fashion replies, "If she truly doesn't accept dialysis or any other interventions, a few days at most." His ghost-like pallor as well as his disregard for her request not to contact me leads me to believe he's being generous in his estimate.

I wrap my head around his words, and my feet carry me back toward her room. How can I fully explain the depth and breadth of our life in a single visit? It's an impossible feat. I step inside her space once again. A simple conversation would be enough. At least I told myself it would be.

"What do you want?" Her question is laced with contempt and disdain that I dared return.

My goal was to share some final words. Instead, I'm met with anger. Rather than I tried or I love you, "Nothing. Goodbye," are the final words I say to her. I march out of the facility without so much as a look back. During the return trip to the hotel, I stare at the passing scenery but don't truly see it.

Not until my suite door latches closed behind me, do I allow myself the grace of feeling the rush of emotions… devastation to pain to relief. I curl up on the king-size duvet and cry for nearly an hour. Why? I'm not sure. Aside from paying for her treatment, I haven't seen her happy or healthy since I was about ten years old. Can you mourn someone who is still alive? My answer is a resounding yes.

This impromptu trip begs a question. Am I required to inform my father?

I haven't spoken to him in nearly four years. He hasn't had a conversation with my mother for much longer. I'm nearing a time where there is only one person for me to rely on in this world. Me. To be fair, I haven't relied on my mother since… but she's family.

I have Kellan, but we're never in the same time zone with my work schedule and his. If we're lucky, we squeeze in a weekend date during the offseason when I'm not filming or Kellan crashes on the couch in my trailer on set. I didn't consult him before booking a flight across the country. A true partner should've been my first call.

These thoughts turn in my mind while I regain my composure. Hours later, I order some food and turn on Kellan's game. Despite the distance in our relationship both literal and figurative, I tune in. As I watch the screen, I don't see him on the field.

Feverishly, I pull up the game details on ESPN. He isn't listed as a starter for today's game. Did he get hurt during warmups? My chest tightens with worry. He was out with an injury last season. Before going deeper down the rabbit hole, I text him. If he's on the bench, his phone will be in the locker room though.

Me: Are you okay?

He answers immediately.

Kellan: Yes. What room are you in?

Me: You're here?

Kellan: Without a doubt.

Me: 1431.

A few minutes later, he knocks on the door. Even in times of distance in our relationship, Kellan shows up for me without fail. We weren't supposed to see each other for another two plus months.

I throw open the door and leap into his arms. No doubt, he'll catch me. The turmoil in my heart doesn't stop me. Once he's inside, I kiss him deeply. Adding space between us, I ask, "How? Why?"

"I requested leave. Coach granted it. You need me here not over there." He points to the screen.

He's right, but…. "Kellan, you have a responsibility to your team."

"I have one to you as well. You sounded distraught. From the look of you, you've been crying hard. Is she—"

I'm about to refute his wording but decide against it. "Not yet." I share the details of my visit this morning.

"Demi. I'm sorry."

I shrug. Nothing really to say. My mother made her decision. Now, I have to wait for the fallout.

For the next day, I jump each instance my phone vibrates with a notification, fearing she's gone. It makes no sense. She isn't nice to me. I can only reconcile her treatment of me with the fact she's ill. The call came in the wee hours of Tuesday morning. By the end of the day, I paid her final bills, arranged for her cremation, and hopped on a flight with Kellan back to our house.

I have limited time to prepare for filming in Australia for two months. The only plus of my mother's death is Kellan's presence. I gained a few more days with him. The notion is bittersweet. I have more hours with him because my mother is dead. Each time we're scheduled to be apart, I mentally prepare myself. I temper my future plans with him, how many calls we'll have, and most importantly, my emotions. I love Kellan with every fiber in my being. However, the ebbs and flows between us make a loving, stable relationship difficult.

I wheel my bag to the foyer and search for Kellan in the house. He's cooling down from a run on the treadmill in our basement gym.

"Leaving?" he asks.

"Yeah."

"Want a ride?"

I shake my head. "I scheduled a car before…."

He drops his head. "Can you ask to push the start of filming?"

I sigh heavily. "I could. What's the point though? It wasn't as if we had a typical mother/daughter relationship. Hell, I was the parent most of my life. The only difference is there won't be any calls. Lily won't reach out for permission to pay another stint in a facility. Our contact wasn't one on one, always through intermediaries."

"I'm sorry."

I wrap my arms around him and absorb the strength he seems to carry in tough situations. "Me too. I'm going to use this time as a break from everything."

His frame stiffens around me. "Even me?"

"Yeah. I think it's necessary for me to get my life back in order with all the changes."

"I don't love this plan. I have firsthand experience in the club you just joined," he admits. Kellan's father died when he was in high school.

I add space between us. "I know. I'm not sure it's right either, but I need a reset for me."

The knock on the front door indicates my driver has arrived.

"Take care of yourself. I love you." Only time will tell if navigating my grief alone is the correct decision.

He kisses the top of my head and replies, "You too."

His failure to share his love means two things. He's hurt and was wholly honest about not being on board with this break. I don't want to throw away our relationship. However, I need time to figure out who I am without parents despite my father still living and breathing somewhere on the planet.

FOUR MONTHS LATER

The premiere for my most recent film is this evening in New York City. Returning to my hometown without a place to lay my head nor anyone to visit is disheartening. Maia from Blackthorne Security is accompanying me.

Exiting the limousine, I scan the crowd. Before my recent movie shoot, I asked Kellan for time to sort out my life. Reluctantly, he agreed. We have restarted taking baby steps toward reuniting again. I'm ecstatic and grateful. The space had nothing to do with him or our relationship.

I walk beside Maia as I make my way along the carpeted walkway. I see the guy move from behind the barrier before she does. He's tall and moderately overweight. Expeditiously, Maia steps between me and Aidan Oaks.

"Demi! Demi! How could you treat him so poorly?" he shouts.

Maia extends her arm and pushes me farther away from Kellan's older brother.

"Sir, go back." She directs and points with her other hand.

"What are you going to do about it? You're a tiny little thing," he goads Maia.

"Sir, behind the rope, please. You don't want to do this in front of these cameras. If you touch me or her, you will be arrested."

"Demi! He did everything you asked, and you dumped him!"

"Sir, go back."

"What are you doing here?" I ask over Maia's shoulder.

"Don't engage him," she mutters under her breath.

A flurry of activity occurs. Two other security personnel approach and lead Aidan off to the office.

Maia leads me directly to a private space so I can regain my composure.

What the hell is Aidan doing here? My relationship with Kellan is none of his business. Sure, they're brothers, but we've never included his family in our day-to-day goings on. The only other family member I've met is his mother. We met at the NFL draft, and we've crossed paths a few times since then. I barely see Kellan, never-mind his family.

"Who is he?" she demands with a hand on her belly to protect her baby.

I shake my head. "Are you okay?"

She sits beside me with a bottled water in hand. "I'm fine. Please don't mention this to Nolan."

I smirk at her. "I won't, but you should. To answer your question, he's my on-again/off-again boyfriend's older brother."

"Who?"

"Kellan Oaks," I reply.

"The football player for DC?" Maia raises an eyebrow in my direction. "Demi, it's my job to be aware who is in your life and where you have concerns. Neither Kellan nor his brother were mentioned in your known associates."

"Kellan and I were private. We had to be, given our age difference."

"Okay. Why is Kellan's brother upset with you?"

"It's complicated. In this business, the time away from home for long periods is a lot to handle. I asked for space to deal with the loss of my mother and my place in this world after losing a parent. I use parent loosely. Kellan accepted my request. That is to say, he didn't love the idea, but he agreed. His family, not so much. I simply needed space to refocus some parts of my life that have nothing to do with him."

Maia nods. "I assume you don't want to press charges."

"No. Aidan is simply fulfilling his older brother duties."

She stands and breathes slowly.

"Are you sure you don't need medical attention?"

Maia shakes her head. "I'm fine. I'll worry about Nolan's reaction later. You ready to sneak into the theater?" Nolan is her fiancé, who also works for Blackthorne. He recently learned he's the first son of the United States after finding out his mother was unfaithful in her marriage.

"Yes."

I sneak into my seat near the front of the room beside my castmates. I'm not too late. Only fifteen minutes of the film have elapsed. I sink as deeply in the cushioned seat as possible. Taking a break was necessary for me. Kellan and I have been easing back into things for the last month. In fact,

I'm going home to him after this event is over. Life in the public eye sucks sometimes.

CHAPTER NINE

KELLAN

PRESENT DAY

The flight to Dallas will only be a few hours. I was shocked when I boarded to find Val already seated.

"You're joining me?"

"Of course. I promised you white-glove service. A three-stop stadium tour will be fun." She grins and buckles her seatbelt.

"Finn let you come alone?" I ask with levity in my tone.

He's her fiancé and works for Blackthorne Security. Val had some issues with a crazed fan last year dating back to her modeling career.

Val laughs heartily and tilts her head toward the rear of the plane. Finn emerges, shakes my hand, and slides into the seat beside her.

"Well played."

Getting to Dallas is bumpy and uncomfortable despite the Pemberton Airlines private plane. Generally, I can handle turbulence, but considering the reason for my air travel as well as the potential… no, probable changes in my personal life, it's fitting. Little did I know the flight would be the beginning of a rough visit.

The ride to the stadium is less than an hour. As we approach, I'm struck by the scaffolds and cranes around the building. Then I recall Val mentioning the upgrades for the World Cup later this year.

"Are you ready for this?" Val asks.

I nod cautiously. "The offer sheet is the middle of the three teams." We exit the blacked-out SUV. Before I can elaborate, we're greeted by the head coach, personnel director, and general manager of the team. They usher Val and I down to the field.

Finn hangs near the tunnel entrance while we talk business. I appreciate his deference and allowing privacy. Given his profession and the nondisclosures he signed when he worked with Demi, he probably knows plenty of details about my contract situation. Interestingly, the executives focus nearly all their statements and questions on me. Val might as well be at her office.

The director of player personnel speaks first. "In all honesty, we need your expertise, Mr. Oaks. We're willing to pay for it, as our contract sheet shows. This team will make you the highest-paid tight end in the league." He believes their team salary is the best on the table. It isn't, partially because we haven't opened negotiations yet. Also, both of my other possible spots have more guaranteed money.

"I appreciate that, but your offer is the starting point. I have two additional teams to look at as well."

He shifts his weight on his feet and glares at the general manager. It would seem they aren't on the same page at all. We continue to discuss the parameters of the contract until the quarterback of the team joins us on the field. Jimmy Dolson is an aging veteran who frankly has his best years behind him. The rumor mill indicated the team was moving on. If I select my new stadium by chances of winning, and he's the leader of the offense, this isn't the team for me.

I muddle through the rest of the meeting, and my suspicions are confirmed. The team has decided to stick with Dolson and beef up his receiving core instead.

My poker face is on point when the head coach asks, "What do you think? Is Dallas still in the running?"

"You've given me a lot to consider. We'll reach out with a decision." I shake their hands and hastily leave the stadium.

Other than polite niceties with Val and the driver, we don't discuss the meeting during the ride back to the airport. We are spending the night in Phoenix ahead of our visit tomorrow.

After, we're ushered into the private lounge. There are wide, plush chairs and a snack bar. I have to admit, Finn is excellent at his job. He's quiet and doesn't talk much. I nearly forgot he was with us. We grab refreshments and take a seat near the floor-to-ceiling windows overlooking the tarmac.

Val asks, "What are your thoughts?" She has my file open in front of her.

I drop my head and consider my words. "Didn't their front office indicate they were overhauling their offense?"

"Yes, or I wouldn't have scheduled the visit."

I believe her. Wasting time on the visit doesn't make sense for either of us. "Understood."

"Off the list?"

I frown. "Most likely."

Four hours later after an uneventful flight, we check into our hotel for the night. It's seven in the evening here.

Our rooms are on the same floor, and we decided on the ride over that room service was in order. As we exit the elevator, Val reminds me. "Our car will be here at ten."

"Thanks. See you then."

My accommodations are more luxurious than normal. The team hotels aren't typically high-end. My room has a king-size bed with luxury bedding and a bathroom to rival any showroom example from the tilework to the black faucets.

I strip off my clothes and don comfy shorts and a tee. Once my dinner order is placed, I video call Demi. While I'm not keen on Dallas. I'm excited to share progress toward finding a new locker room to hang my helmet.

"Hi!" she answers immediately. Even from afar, my body reacts to her. She's wearing a thin yoga shirt with a tank beneath it. The slope of her neck and collarbone is exposed. My deep-rooted need to drag my tongue along her skin is intense despite the fact it's been years since I've held her at all.

"Hey."

Demi is quiet for a moment and then she asks, "How did the first team visit go?"

I share the details of the day from the construction to the fact they aren't retooling their offense.

She frowns. "That sucks. Why not be honest? It isn't a good look overall."

I acknowledge her statement. "I agree. Obviously, Dallas isn't a great option. We shall see what tomorrow brings. What have you been up to today?"

Her shoulders drop slightly and then she grins. "I've been pulling together my schedule for the next two years."

I'm dumbstruck. Numerous emotions cascade through me. Is it possible Demi heard me? I'm cautiously optimistic but still worried our time together will be the same as before. My last-chance edict is firm. I want a family. I want to build a home and children… with her. Can we really make a go of our final try? Book me a space on cloud nine if that's the case.

"Please share what you're thinking out loud. I won't run. I've spent a lot many hours rehashing where things flipped pear-shaped since we started talking again. More specifically, accepting the blame for not trying hard enough for us."

"I'm grateful you see where we went wrong before."

Demi is rarely at a loss for words. She inhales sharply and looks to the side. Surprise and discomfort mar her gorgeous face. Even without makeup, Demi is stunning. In fact, fresh-faced is my favorite version of her. Sure, a slinky, designer dress always works. Everyday Demi is sweet, fun, and when we're in the same place, she's attentive and doting.

"What don't you agree with?" I ask.

She tugs her lower lip between her teeth. The move normally stirs a response in me, but not when she's on the verge of tears. The one thing I own is reading her true emotions. I'm probably the only person who can tell when she's acting and when her genuine emotions are surfacing. Now is absolutely the latter.

Demi exhales slowly and replies, "You can be honest with me, Kellan. We didn't go wrong before. The blame falls mostly on me."

"I appreciate your position, but if we're becoming a team again, we bear the burdens and joys equally regardless of fault."

I love you. Those words echo in my mind. This moment is certainly not the time to share them with Demi.

"Thank you."

Her response is short but feels heavy. Demi owning most of the weight of our topsy-turvy relationship eases some of my angst. As much as I love her and want to spend the rest of my life with her, I don't want to be devastated again. My heart won't survive. "You're welcome."

Deafening silence rushes between us for a few minutes. Demi uses the time to regain her composure. To be honest, I'm saved by a knock on my door.

"Be right back. I need to get my dinner." I don't wait for her to respond. I accept my meal, sign the slip, and set up the table before resetting my phone. I decline the waiter's offer to enter and complete this task. I may have means, but I'm not fussy. Certain things I spend money on. Normally, room service isn't one of them.

I take a bite of my chicken. Finally, my stomach may stop growling at me.

"I'm back. What else have you been up to?"

She smiles weakly. Her emotions are splayed on her face. "Relaxing mostly. I have been working without a break for the last six months. Tomorrow, I plan to focus on business stuff. I need to cull the designers for the presentation and talk with Celeste about the press schedule before the awards shows and the nominee luncheon."

"A week is a big deal for you," I admit.

"Yeah, it is. I needed to slow down though."

Despite my fear, I ask, "When does your next movie start?"

Demi tilts her head. "About a week after the Oscar Awards. I'm filming in Hollywood." If I recall, the ceremony is in March.

Close by. Perhaps we could make us work. I polish off my dinner and two bottles of water. "Not bad. You have about a month." It's plenty of time for us to see if the spark is still there and how to navigate a life together before she goes to film and I find a new place to lay my head at night unless it's LA.

I'm itching to talk about us more, but I intend to respect her wishes. Face-to-face is the way to go. "I'm beat. I'll call you tomorrow after the visit."

"Night, Kellan." She blows me a kiss.

“Sweet dreams,” I reply and end the call. After wheeling the table into the hall, I get ready for bed. Hopefully, Phoenix is better than Dallas.

Just before ten the next morning, I meet Val and Finn in the lobby of the hotel.

“Round two,” I state, and we ride to the stadium. This facility has been renovated less recently than the others I will tour in my search for a new team. The building age isn’t a dealmaker or breaker for me. As long as I mesh with the quarterback, head coach, and offensive coordinator, I can make the rest work. *Ideally, with Demi beside me.*

The vibe here is much better than yesterday. We’re greeted by the team executives and receive a tour of the facility ending with the newly replaced turf.

On the far end, two players are warming up.

Val mutters beside me, “Now the front office’s insistence makes complete sense.”

“What does?” I look over at her. With her stilettos on, she’s nearly eye to eye with me.

“Can you see them?”

I shake my head. “Not enough to make out who they are?”

“Why?”

“I hoped to have this visit first, but the team was adamant about you showing up today.”

“Okay?” A hint of “so what” is in my tone.

She raises her arm and urges me forward. As I approach, I recognize the smooth motion of the receiver in stride as he catches a simple toss. Jordan? Here?

As I get closer, my steps increase in speed. Val falls back. I appreciate her giving me space.

"Dude!" I greet him with a bro hug. Then I realize the entire DC trifecta is on this turf. For the first time in too long, joy and childlike excitement swells in my chest. "Press, good to see you as well, man." We fly through our carefully honed handshake before hugging. A bond like ours forged in blood, sweat, injuries, and rings is for life.

Well, it seems I could be reunited with my former teammates Preston Jameson and Jordan Devereaux. Press is a seventh-year quarterback with two rings. Jordan has two rings as well. One we earned together.

We chat while Press throws easy passes to the two of us.

"Why are you looking for a new home?" My question is directed at them.

Press answers first, "I need offensive weapons, and well, DC isn't going to provide them especially if they aren't keeping you. The front office traded Jordan and my running back last year. Now you're on the block this season. I hate struggling to be at the bottom of the league."

Jordan tosses the ball back to him, then he adds, "My family isn't thriving as well as we would've liked in Atlanta. We were used to suburban areas, perhaps closer to rural life outside of DC with great friends and found family. As evidenced by your presence," he motions between both Press and me, "going home isn't an option. What about you?" Jordan and his wife,

Alex, have two kids, an older daughter, Reese, who must be in middle school by now, and a young son named Rowan.

"I'm old."

Both Press and Jordan laugh. I've been in the league a few more years than both.

I continue, "It's true. This will likely be my last contract. I want to win, and staying in DC is the fastest way for my dream of another ring to die."

"True dat," Press adds. He's obviously of the same mindset as he's shopping his golden arm.

Could the three of us end up here? Playing together again? Clearly, the front office believes it could happen. We've won as a unit before. Cautious joy zips from my head to my toes. The feeling doesn't last long. Fear creeps in. Not about my boys, but regarding Demi. Rather than stew on my concerns, I stick with the happiness for now. I still have one more team on my list. On paper, LA would seem to be the best for my relationship while this one leads to my professional future. *Damn!*

We bullshit for another hour while laughing and chucking the ball around. We both run downfield at once. Finn steps in and tosses an out route to me while Press hits Jordan on a slant.

"Did you play?" I ask Finn when I return to the twenty-yard line. Preston and Jordan are high-fiving each other.

He shrugs. "Just for fun and during the Blackthorne flag game on Thanksgiving."

"All right."

“You up for catching a meal, or do you need to hightail it out to your next stop?” Preston asks.

I frown. “Unfortunately, the latter.”

The three of us agree to reach out before making final decisions. We exit at once. I return to the airport while the guys have dinner first.

I’m torn. Professionally, Press, Jordan, and I could make a run in Arizona together. While I have another team to interview, Phoenix is looking like the most promising option. Can Demi and I make it if here is the best spot to win?

CHAPTER TEN

DEMI

New grass will be required if I don't sit down. I've been pacing back and forth since Kellan's text. He left the stadium. The actual distance is less than thirty miles. However, traffic in the Los Angeles metro area is nuts, all day, every day.

The reality of him in the same room as me after more than four years is insane. Our last rendezvous was intense and filled with pleasure. Today is a different story. My emotions are scattered. Nervous energy rushes through me on my first step and then anxiety on the next. Aside from Kellan being on his way here, he didn't mention how the visit went at all. Not knowing adds to my stress. Of the three teams, LA is the closest and would make the most sense time and distance-wise. His former teammates, Jordan and Preston are considering Arizona as well. While I'm not Howie Long or Michael Strahan, my football knowledge is extensive. He would have an excellent chance to reach the big game again with Arizona. I want the opportunity for him.

A strong knock on my front door crashes into my thoughts. *He's here!* I step toward my front door while breathing deeply. My hand trembles as I lower the handle.

Kellan is…. I'm awestruck. How is it possible he's hotter now? The man is aging like fine wine. His chiseled jaw remains the same. He's leaner than during our fling after Madeleine's wedding. A signature scent he's worn for years wafts in my direction.

His green eyes bore into mine, and he says, "Hi, Dolce."

My insides turn gooey, and I mumble, "You're really here?"

A wide grin graces his face. "Yes. Can I come in?"

With a shake of my head, I step to the side and watch him enter my home for the first time. *Damn!* He may be thinner, but his strong thighs still make my mouth water. A memory of him pinning me against a wall in my luxurious suite at the Anderson wedding flashes through my mind.

Kellan stops a few steps in and extends his hand in my direction. When I don't immediately take it, he retraces his steps and stands before me.

"What are you afraid of?" he whispers as he looks down at me. The height difference without heels is markedly larger.

"Failing us again."

"Good." He bends, curls his arm around my waist and draws me close.

Warmth and, dare I say, love surround me. Falling for Kellan again would be so easy. Hell, I never stopped loving him. With each second in his arms, the good memories rush back. For a few minutes, he holds me as if I didn't obliterate his heart earlier in our relationship.

When I stop cataloging how I feel in his embrace and the comfort, I process his response to my earlier statement. I frown and pull back to stare at him. "What do you mean good?"

"Sharing our fears is the first step to pulling off a future together. Did you change your mind?"

A thrill passes over me. Kellan is in this too. "No, not at all."

"Me either." He leans forward to kiss me. A hairsbreadth of space is between our lips.

As much as I yearn to strip his clothes off, I lean back slightly. "We never had issues in the sexy time department."

He clears his throat. The bulge against me is unmistakable. Kellan lowers me to the floor. "No, we didn't." He adjusts himself.

To break the tension a bit, I ask, "Would you like a drink?"

"Sure."

He follows me into the kitchen, and I share what I have on hand.

"Water is fine for now," he replies without looking at me. "Your home is stunning."

"Thank you. How was the visit?"

His shoulders fall. His reaction makes me believe LA isn't the place for him.

"We need to put it all out there." I extend my hand to him and lead him to the patio.

He's in awe of Point Dume in my backyard. "Is there where you were sitting when we talked?"

"One of the times, yeah."

"Beautiful."

"I love it. This house is large, but it provides privacy, hiking trails, and this extraordinary view." We take seats and stare at the scenery instead of each other.

A few minutes later, Kellan shares details of his stop in LA. "The facilities are state of the art. The front office staff was courteous. Their offense is upper third of the league."

I hear the underlying dismay with the visit. "But?"

He turns and looks at the side of my face. Tilting slightly, I meet his gaze. "How do you…?"

"You are… were… are…," I shake off the discomfort, "I know you. We've had some major bumps in our relationship. I'm confident the visit didn't go as you would've liked."

"It should have. It's the closest to you, and the initial offer is near what I'm worth."

I stand and move to the bottom of his chaise. Kellan sits up and places one foot on either side of the chair. I sit on the bottom facing him. "I don't have the right to ask anymore, but…."

"You do. If we're going to work, you can ask anything of me. Whether or not it's sensible is something else."

I tug my lower lip between my teeth before adding, "Promise me… pick the best place for you, not me."

He pauses too long for my liking. "I can't."

My shoulders fall. “How do we make progress if you won’t meet me halfway?” I pull my lips into a tight line. I raise my hand to stop him. “Don’t answer yet. I’ll be right back.”

I hurry to my office and grab the schedule I created. It’s ten typed pages and covers the next two years. I hand him the stack of papers and sit closer than I was before.

“What’s this?”

“It’s my work life. The only part missing is yours. I downloaded the game schedule for the three teams you visited. Once you choose the best spot for you, we add them in.”

He frowns and peruses the pages. Quietly he flips through. “You weren’t kidding?”

“No. You never failed us. I did. I appreciate you bearing some of the weight, but the culprit was me. Instead of choosing to do the hard work, I pushed you away.”

He inhales sharply, before adding, “I let you. I didn’t own the issues we were having either.”

I shrug.

He looks down at the sheets in his hand again. Now, he’s actually reading the words on the page. “You blocked off space for us, games, visits to set, and then some.” Time on Sundays for games at least.

“Yes. I want us to do it right. We need to work together and be with each other even if it’s for a day.”

“What’s different now?”

My heart is in my throat and tears threaten to fall. "I didn't know what a strong, stable relationship looked like. You do. You tried to show me. I should've listened."

Kellan slides his hand up and cups my face. I press into his palm. The touch of his skin on mine makes my heart rate jump. Always has. "Our breakup was on both of us. Neither you nor I put any energy toward a solution. We took the coward's way out."

"It wasn't easy. Not at all," I blurt.

He shakes his head. "It was torture. When I saw your key on the island, I nearly hurled on the tile floor."

"I dialed six numbers so many times." The Garth Brooks song with that line plays in my head. "More than a Memory," I think it's called. "I texted an equal amount but never sent them."

Kellan reaches forward and hauls me into his arms. He kisses my temple and replies, "Me too."

Safety and comfort surround me, and I mumble against his rock-hard chest, "What do we do now?"

Before he can answer, his phone rings.

"I'll check later," he murmurs softly.

"It could be Val," I remind him.

Kellan shifts, plucks his phone from his pocket and answers, "Hi, Val."

I attempt to move to offer privacy, but his arm tightens around me.

I can hear her clearly.

Val states, "I have a few updates for you. Dallas has upped their offer to fifteen million guaranteed with no change over the rest of the contract. Arizona's offer is thirty-five million guaranteed up front and five million a year for five years."

Whoa! Good for him.

He relaxes slightly as Val continues, "LA was impressed with you. They top out at twenty-eight guaranteed and six million for four seasons."

"Thanks, Val. I need to think this over. Did the teams give a deadline?"

Shuffling papers comes through the phone before she replies, "Three days, tops."

"Please email me the offer sheets."

Val laughs. "Tate already did."

"He's on point as usual."

"Yes. I thank Simon for finding him almost daily."

"I'll reach out with my decision soon." He ends the call and stares upward.

"Ready to talk more or want to discuss with Press and Jordan first?" I ask.

Kellan lowers his gaze to meet mine. "I missed you, Dolce. You were… are…."

"I'm still your best friend. We just took a break from offering advice and kudos for a little while. A bond like ours doesn't disappear."

"You always had my back even when I wrongly thought otherwise."

"You did for me as well."

Kellan kisses my forehead, and I narrowly resist sighing. The intimacy isn't lost on me. Forcing myself to go slow is another story.

"Do you have food, or do we need to order dinner?" he asks.

"Carol hooked us up. If you don't like the options, we can opt for takeout in."

"I'm glad someone has been feeding you since you returned. You're too thin."

I shake my head. Kellan always made sure I ate well. He never subscribed to the skinny is better school of thought. "The food on set for my last film was terrible. Only when I was able to explore a bit was the cuisine worth it. I survived mostly on protein shakes and fruit. I requested comfort food when I got home. Carol's lasagna and chicken pot pie are amazing."

As if on cue, Kellan's stomach growls.

We laugh and pad to the kitchen. He stands in front of the fridge and asks for permission to check.

"Please make yourself at home."

"Feels a bit awkward is all."

I set my hand on his tight, muscled forearm. Heat zips to my heart. "It is. Hopefully, the discomfort will pass soon."

He opens both doors and peruses the contents. I set the oven to cook the lasagna. It's his favorite.

I giggle when he sets the aluminum baking dish on the Carrara island.

"You knew?"

"No question in my mind. You might as well be Garfield when it comes to this Italian dish."

"Are you even old enough to know who the feisty feline is?"

"Hardy har har." It's nice to laugh again and mean it. Our age gap was never an issue for me personally. However, it was viewed as a problem when we met, which led us to be cautious. The weirdness is bound to disappear. Right?

CHAPTER ELEVEN

KELLAN

She's stunning. That was the first thing that came to mind when her front door swung open. How could she possibly be more beautiful now than when we met? Even casually dressed in leggings and an off-the-shoulder top, she's… perfect. While the initial entry was weird, holding her is miles better than before. Demi in my arms will never be matched.

Standing in her kitchen cracking jokes, the tension has eased somewhat. I'm hesitant to trust our connection and restart our relationship despite knowing with every fiber in my being we're meant to be.

Her typed schedule was thorough. Before… we were winging it month to month. Demi planned out the next two years, including me attending the Oscars with her. I didn't mention it before when I skimmed the pages, but I'm excited she wants me on her arm. While I'm successful in my chosen profession, I'm man enough to acknowledge and accept she's on the upswing of her career while I'm on the back end.

"Kellan." Her calling me breaks into my thoughts.

"Yeah?"

"You okay?" she asks. Demi stares until I answer.

"I need the discomfort to go away. Please don't get me wrong, I want to be here, but it's…."

“Not like before?” she suggests to fill in my thoughts.

“Exactly. This time feels—”

“Heavier,” Demi interrupts, “and it’s scary as hell.”

In two steps, I eliminate the space between us, cup her face, and press my lips to hers. Fireworks and a rush of lust pulse through my body. Our tongues tangle and fight for supremacy. I slide my hands lower, lift her onto the island, and step between her thighs. Her fingers thread into my hair and tug slightly.

Missed her. Missed my person knowing my preferences. A surge of heat points southward.

Demi grips the back of my shirt and tugs it over my head.

“Damn, Kellan!”

My cheeks flush, and I take the opportunity to toss her shirt aside.

“You should talk.” I lower my mouth to the sweet-smelling valley between her ample breasts. Then I lick my way up her chin and back to her plump lips.

We kiss until we’re both panting for breath.

“Holy hell!”

I grin at her. “Never had issues with showing affection. Did we?”

“No.”

In novels and movies, they say a kiss will tell you everything you need to know. The last few with Demi give me hope. Perhaps we can actually pull off a future together.

We right our clothes, or in my case, tug my shirt back on, and wash up. With heaping helpings of lasagna, we sit at the dining table and dig in.

In between bites, I ask, “How often does Carol cook for you?”

Demi wrinkles her nose. “She comes once or twice a week when I’m home to prepare meals and tidy up. Why?”

“Think she’ll share her recipe with me?”

A huge smile grows on her face. “Probably will.”

“Good.”

“Any news to catch me up on other than football?” Demi asks.

“Not really. We’ve been talking about everything except that until now.”

She inhales sharply.

“Don’t take it personally. I understood and agreed to wait to discuss my landing spot after the visits and in person.”

Her shoulders drop back to normal slowly. “Okay.”

“Not convincing, Dolce.”

“As much as I appreciate you sharing some of the blame from our past failures, it was mostly on me. The reason I left hasn’t changed. The time available for us to be in the same place is limited.”

“But?” I mutter under my breath.

“I’ve changed. I need you to trust me. It’s a huge ask. I understand completely if you’re hesitant. I’m all in for us. I don’t take your ultimatum lightly. I will be better. I will show up for you like you have for me in the past.”

"I do trust you." I pause before admitting my fears. "I'm terrified we won't figure out how to make a relationship work between two high-achieving professionals without one of us sacrificing too much."

Demi covers my hands with her. She tries to, at least. "We will."

I look up and stare into her eyes. A fierceness for us is present. Hope and joy rush through me. I've only seen it for her career. Perhaps this time can be forever. I lower my head and kiss her hands. "Let's clean up and see how two of the teams fit into your schedule."

She adamantly states, "You should choose Arizona, especially if Jordan and Preston plan to do the same."

That is my preferred spot. Only if it's the three of us. "Perhaps true, but LA isn't out of the running just yet."

"Fair enough." We quickly wash our dishes. Then she leads me to her office. It's to the right of the front entryway. It has floor-to-ceiling bookcases in soft ivory. The desk and furnishings are a deep charcoal tone with pops of color on the tufted sofa and chairs.

"Go ahead. Take a seat. I'll fire up the printer," she urges.

I comply and open her laptop. She tugs on a cabinet door behind me to the left, and a few steady beeps echo in the quiet space.

"What's your password?"

"Knockout," she replies.

I press the keys and recall the reasons she gave me the nickname. It's a take on my initials, but she was also knocked off her feet when we met. Her words, not mine. "You never changed it?"

"No. Did you?" Perhaps we can make it after all this time. Neither of us ever gave up on our relationship.

I shake my head and then refocus on the screen. My password for my phone and laptop is still Dolce. I log into my email. "All set?"

"Should be."

I press print, and a whirring sound begins behind me. "Do you have the schedules saved, or do I need ESPN?"

She grins at me. "There's a folder on the desktop with your name. The schedules for all three are in there."

I navigate to the folder labelled Kellan and print two of the three. Dallas is definitely off the table for me. There are three documents, one for each team in addition to the schedule.

"Why don't you call the guys?" Demi suggests.

"It's late," I reply.

"They will answer because it's you."

Preston is in DC, and Jordan is in Atlanta. "Good point. I will. Thanks."

She nods and exits her home office. I send a joint text instead.

Me: You up to chat?

I don't expect instant answers. While I wait, I stare out the large window toward Demi's front yard. The landscaping is pristine and soothing, much like the view in the rear. Then I recall the extra files. I click the one for LA. There is a pro and con list, including proximity and access to an international airport. She also broke down the schedule and opponents. At the bottom of the page, she left the overall analysis blank. Intrigued, I select

Arizona. I'm floored. The same information with different entries is included. The positives include higher chance of winning another ring and the team offense structure is set for me. She didn't note any negatives. Not even moving from her home? Is she willing to give this up for me? At the bottom of the page, her summary has one single sentence. "This is the best team for Kellan." *Trust her words and actions.* She created this schedule. Demi laid herself out there in multiple pages. I need to own my fears. Arizona is first, and then LA, as far as landing spots.

Preston Jameson: Yes.

JDevereaux: Same here.

I dial Jordan and conference Preston in.

"Hey!" Preston shouts.

"What's up?" I answer.

Jordan jumps right in. "How was LA?"

I don't mince words. These guys are my brothers. They want what's best for me even if it isn't on the same roster as them. "Not terrible. Dallas is off the table though. What about you guys?"

Preston answers, "Arizona is my top choice. Tennessee is a distant second. JDev?"

"Full disclosure, I'm torn. Denver is also a great fit for me," my friend admits.

"I did an analysis. We could win with the three of us back together. There would be two road games, which would be tough. Only one is in our division." Preston is a film fiend. Once he's done dissecting the offense of our weekly opponent, he would pick apart their games from previous weeks or dig into a coach's history to look for tendencies.

"What is Alex's opinion?" I ask Jordan. Alex is his wife. She gave up her career to follow him. I would never ask Demi to do the same for me, especially since she wouldn't allow me to retire for her.

Jordan drops his head. "She prefers the team where I can reach the big game again."

"Why do you think Denver will be better?" Preston asks.

"It would be for Alex and the kids. Plus, the defense is solid… top ten in the league last season."

He isn't wrong. "I understand where you're coming from."

"Back on again?" Press asks. These two were on the tiny list of people who knew about my relationship status over the years.

"Maybe." I pause to consider my words carefully. Then I realize I don't have to. "I've been in a similar spot as you are right now, Jordan. The main difference is Alex already gave up her career. I agree with Press. The three of us together again in a warmer climate would be what Super Bowl dreams are made of."

"We have a few more days, right?" Jordan asks.

"Yeah," I reply.

Jordan drags his hand down his face. He's truly torn. He has permission to choose the better team, and he's on the fence. The only difference between him and me is trust in her consent. Well, that and a wedding band. "I'll talk this out with Alex more and get back to you both."

"Later man," I say, and Jordan leaves the call.

Preston asks, "What about you?"

I hesitate only for a moment. If Demi and I are going to make it long term, I need to be happy with this decision. I need to trust her. "Arizona is the best spot for me."

"Same. Hopefully, JDev will come around."

"Yeah. Later, Press."

He hangs up. Now, I need to tell Demi and mesh our schedules together. I gather the papers and search for her. If memory serves, she's likely curled up in her bed reading.

Rather than shout, I walk down the hall to the left of the kitchen. There are three bedrooms with an en suite bathroom and a laundry room. Passing through the main space, which is spacious and comfortable, I find it's closed up for the night. The house is a mirror image on either side of the living area only. This wing has the master bedroom, his and hers walk-in closets, a massive bathroom and private sitting room. I find Demi snuggled in a chair in the master. I can see her messy bun over the back.

"Demi," I state as I approach to avoid startling her. Either she doesn't hear me or she's asleep. Setting my hand on her shoulder Demi nearly jumps out of the curved chair.

She plucks her earbuds out of her ears. "Hey."

"Sorry, I scared you. Were you listening or reading?"

"The latter. I wanted to give you privacy, and silence helps me stay focused on the book."

"If it isn't good, don't finish it."

She laughs heartily. "I don't love this novel, but I'm set to star in the screen adaptation. Well, I need to get into the author's head or at least try to."

"Maybe you shouldn't do the film if the book is terrible," I offer as unsolicited advice.

"It isn't bad. I'm not focused is all. How are Preston and Jordan?"

I shrug and update her on the call, including my new home.

Demi leaps up and throws her arms around me. "I'm crazy happy for you, Kellan."

"Thanks. Are you up for adding in the games now, or does tomorrow work?"

"I'm sure you're exhausted from the trip. Over breakfast is fine. I can show you to the guest room."

I shake my head. "I found them while I was looking for you. Any preference which I choose?"

Demi smiles. "The middle one has a king-sized bed. You will be most comfortable there."

I would rather stay here with you. True, it's been a long time since we've shared a bed, but baby steps don't make sense with Demi. I explored and kissed every inch of her for more than a decade. This last span was a few years, but even during our fling, we slept together. I won't push her. Instead, I lean in and kiss her lighter than earlier in the kitchen. I refuse to take steps backward now.

"Goodnight, Dolce."

"Night, Kellan."

I leave quickly before I do something stupid. Despite our past, she's my best friend and the woman I want to be with for the rest of my life. If she needs a night to catch up, fine with me.

I wash up and climb into the ultra-soft, fresh-smelling sheets and stare at the ceiling fan. I'm at least two thousand rotations and counting when there's a gentle knock on the door.

I sit up, and the sheets pool in my lap. Demi is standing in the doorway. Her legs are on full display in her tiny shorts.

"Everything okay?"

"Yes. No," she replies.

"Talk to me," I encourage her.

"It's weird having you here," she motions to her house in general, "but not there." She points toward her bedroom, I think.

Before I consider the ramifications, I slide to the right and throw the sheets open for her to join me.

Demi crosses the room, removes her hoodie, and climbs into bed with me. Without further hesitation or worry, I draw her close and kiss her shoulder blade. Her silky pajamas barely cover her. They're a blessing and a curse in one outfit. Willing my body to ignore her firm ass against me is impossible.

Once I finish shifting my thoughts by focusing on a boring, not sexy image of the uniform bin postgame, I whisper, "Better?"

"Much."

I agree and close my eyes. It won't take long for sleep to claim me with her safely ensconced in my arms.

CHAPTER TWELVE

KELLAN

JANUARY 2021

The final game of the season and we lost handily to a division rival. I throw the contents of my locker in a spare bag on the carpeted floor. The silence in the dressing room is deafening. This season was a bust of epic proportions. The only positive is I'm moderately healthy. Most of my teammates can't say the same. The wideout has a shattered ankle, the right tackle is saddled with a torn pectoral muscle, and the quarterback has a separated shoulder. Our performance doesn't help my chances in securing a long-term contract for next year or anything longer.

Veterans and former players claim retirement whispers in your ear. Am I done with the game I love? I hope not. Would walking away allow me to pursue a family with Demi? Yes, without question. My recovery after games has taken a hit, but I can manage it. I toss the last item into the duffle. Zipping the bag draws attention. The guys around me pause from their cleanup and offer a handshake or a bro hug. I may not see some of these players again.

"Good luck, man," the injured kicker states.

The burly lineman swallows me up in his beefy arms, and I'm not a small dude. "See you on the flip side."

The average career in the NFL is slightly more than three years. I've been in Seattle for the last six years and injury free for five seasons. Lucky is an understatement. The clock is ticking for me both physically and with the young talent joining the ranks from college.

As I exit the stadium, I exchange well-wishes with the staff as I walk along the corridor, probably for the last time. I knew leaving would be difficult. It's one reason I asked Demi to go home at the end of the game rather than wait for me in the tunnel. This contest is one of the rare occasions she has been able to attend. Her filming schedule is nuts, to be fair. I suppose being one of the most sought-after actresses in Hollywood will do that. Her popularity and skill set make a stable homelife difficult. The reality is… she's never home for more than a few weeks span. The chance we're sleeping in our bed at once is less likely. There have been instances where she chose to stay away because one night or event wasn't worth the travel. I felt… I wasn't worth the time and effort.

After the hours I spent in the locker room post-game, the traffic is minimal. Pressing the button, my garage door opens, and I pull inside. The thunk of my heavy bags hitting the floor in the laundry room echoes in my mind. I'm torn between the game I've loved since peewee football and the woman that makes my heart soar. Demi is the love of my life. I want to establish a loving home, have a few kids, and grow old with her. Making us work has been harder than I anticipated.

When I step inside, Demi greets me. "Want to talk or eat?"

Normally, after a game when we're both home, we dissect what went wrong and right to make the following week better. This season is over. Discussing the details of how horrible it was can wait. "We should discuss the season and us, but I need sleep."

Demi takes my hand and leads me toward our bedroom. Despite our time together being short, she agrees to wait to consider my future. My gorgeous, talented girlfriend leaves to shoot two movies back-to-back tomorrow afternoon without a break in between. Our plan is for me to meet her between films for a two-week vacation in Europe rather than her flying to and from the States. Overall, she will be working for nearly four months straight. I understand. I don't begrudge her the success. The schedule itself is horrible.

She slips between our sheets, throws back the covers on my side, and turns to become the little spoon. It would be comical for her to attempt to be the big spoon. She may be tall for a woman, but I still dwarf her by four inches and one hundred and fifty pounds of finely-honed muscle.

I curl my arm around her, draw her body against mine, and kiss the top of her shoulder. "Love you, Dolce."

"I love you."

Bright and early the next morning after a restless night's sleep, I find Demi's side of the bed cold and empty. Turning off my thoughts and worries was impossible.

I pad around our home until I find her sipping a large cup of coffee on the rear patio.

"Morning." I lean down and kiss her forehead. "I'll grab a cup and join you."

She smiles, but it doesn't quite reach her eyes. A shift in her emotional state happens each time Demi gears up to leave for work. I get it. I go through it too. The distance for her films is difficult to navigate, but worth it.

A little while later, I sit beside her looking out at the water view behind our home. Technically, it belongs to me, but it's for us.

"You mentioned you wanted to talk before the game. What's on your mind, babe?" she asks.

I take a deep breath, and without glancing at her, I reply, "I'm considering retirement rather than searching for a new team." I risk turning my head to gauge her reaction to my words.

Fire explodes in her gaze. Yet, she doesn't respond forcefully. "How long have you been thinking about hanging up your helmet? Why?"

"At least this entire season, probably more. I want a family. I need time with you and the ability to care for our children while you work to pull it off."

I see the anger bubbling inside her. She sets down her mug and shifts to face me. Then she begins wringing her hands in her lap. It's one of her few tells. She's anxious and upset about this conversation. "You didn't share before now because?"

I bracket her thighs with mine and slowly separate her hands before threading our fingers together. "I wasn't sure. As the season wore on, my opinion became clear as Lake Tahoe… you are my future. I could suit up as long as my talent and body will allow. Then what? Broadcasting? Real estate sales like Darius? Nothing wrong with either of those, but I don't need to work. I've invested well, and my business portfolio is thriving. Playing has become more of a job than pursuing my passion for the sport. I suppose losing desire is an inevitable fact. Right? Realizing you're human and not Superman." Surprisingly, I expect my heart to ache sharing my epiphany with Demi. It doesn't. In fact, I feel somehow lighter. Briefly, anyway.

"I can't let you forgo your dream of winning a Superbowl for me."

"Sweetheart, I don't want more money or a ring. I need you beside me every single morning for the rest of my life. I need a gorgeous daughter with your eyes and my charm and a sweet boy who loves his mom. "

Tears threaten to plummet down her cheeks. "I can't start a family right now, Kellan. I have contracts that require me to look a certain way. A baby bump doesn't fit in my life for at least three years."

"That's fine. If I retire, I can travel to your filming locations. It gives us more time than we have now."

"Truly, I want as many minutes as we can cobble together, but proximity isn't going to change the number of free moments I have. There's always a scene that gets moved or weather issues that impact the timeline."

The insides of my body feel like they're on display for the world to see. I'm gutted. I manage to whisper, "Do you want to be mine?"

Demi cups my face and replies, "Yes."

There is no hesitation or shred of doubt in her succinct response.

"But?" I mumble. It's a wonder she hears me.

"I refuse to let you quit for me. I love you. I want to be with you forever." Her eyes clamp closed briefly before she adds, "I can't live with the resentment that is bound to occur later in our life if you choose me over football." She bites on her lower lip to quell the tears, but she fails. "I love that you are willing to sacrifice your dream for mine… but…." Demi lifts her chin toward the sky and takes in a shaky breath. "I won't let you."

My heart shatters into a million tiny pieces. Each shard holds a memory of us together. "Where do we go from here?" I mutter under my breath, hoping she doesn't hear me. The next words from her lips obliterate the life I have planned for us.

"I need to leave for these films, and we are done. It's the only chance you won't do something crazy and stupid like retiring for time. Time I can't give you."

My eyes clamp closed as I swallow hard to force the bile and vomit back where it belongs. Despite the revolt happening in my body, I calmly reply, "I'll get out of your way. I wish you the best."

My words aren't a lie, but they feel hollow in this moment. Without a touch, kiss, or even a look back, I leave her sitting on our patio. Hastily, I throw on some clothes. When I pass where I left her, Demi is gone. The only sign of her presence this morning is the cup in the kitchen sink and the lacerations on my heart. I exit my home and start driving without a destination in mind.

An hour later, I find myself at Mt. Baker-Snoqualmie Park. They have trails and beautiful mountain views. If I were brave enough, I could go caving. Definitely not today. I glance at the trail map and shake my head. My trail choices are Happy Creek or Independence Lake. Nowhere else for me to deal with my emotions right now. I can't use my home gym, and the facility is closed. At some other time, this might be funny. Perhaps it will be when I look back years in the future. I opt for the shorter distance and shuffle to the trailhead for Independence Lake.

Hoping to ignore my emotions for a little while, I take off running without a warm-up. It's foolish, but I don't care. To add to the stupidity, my body aches from the hits I took yesterday. My footfalls are heavy and increase the punishment I endured between the lines. At most, I should be stretching and getting a massage.

She loves me but doesn't want me to choose her. I shake my head. Demi doesn't want me with her on set. I'm confident she isn't lying about her free time. Hearing it out loud was a different story.

Will I resent her later in our life together? I don't believe so, but how does one truly know their reactions years in advance? I hoped to parse out my feelings with each step, but I fail. When I reach the end of the trail, I feel no better than I did when I showed up.

The text on my phone when I returned to my truck didn't help either.

Dolce: Take care of yourself, Kellan. I love you.

It takes restraint not to throw my phone out the window and wait for another vehicle to smash it into bits. Her words and actions don't match.

Breaking up a nearly six-year long relationship without more than one conversation is unacceptable. Yet here we are.

To me, her text indicates she left the house. I confirm by watching her pull out of my driveway via my security app on my phone. Exhausted both physically and mentally, I start my truck and drive home.

That word strikes me hard. A home was the one thing we were never able to pull off. While we shared space when we were able, the four walls were a place for us to lay our heads. We weren't able to always be in the space at once. Time was a central issue in our relationship. There was never enough to build the home and family I crave.

I refuse to allow myself to have less than I deserve. My parents provided a lofty example of marriage despite its short tenure. A similar partnership is my only goal. Seems to me, I need to start over if Demi and I are truly done.

The ride is shorter on the way home given the hour. As expected, her space in the garage is empty. I was ready to see her luxury SUV gone. I was not prepared to see her key on the kitchen island. Running my finger over the piece of metal made this seem more real. I had a tangible item to prove she's gone. It was only the first shred of proof.

Overall, we kept our space clutter-free. Our personal items were confined to the office and the bedroom. When I cross the threshold, I see her dresser-drawers open and empty. Half of the walk-in closet is barren and devoid of any indication Demi lived here at all.

Devastated and with visual evidence, I crawl into our bed for the rest of the day. Should I have showered first? Absolutely. Truth is… there's no one around to care anymore.

My isolation lasts a few days before Darius shows up and kicks my butt toward living again. I'm grateful for him. He's the sole reason I pull myself together and end up earning a ring under my next contract.

CHAPTER THIRTEEN

DEMI

JUNE 2021

You are cordially invited to the wedding of Madeleine Wilton and Christoph Anderson.

I read the invitation more than once. Happy doesn't begin to cover my feelings about this event. Well, I'm ecstatic for my agent and her husband-to-be. There's only one person I want to attend this party with, but we have miles of baggage between us.

Me: Hey. Long time, no talk. How are you?

I'm not expecting a response. I toss the remaining mail on the island and continue on with my day. After a workout and shower, I check my phone again. A perk of my profession is my agent handles nearly all my phone calls. This number is known to approximately five people. I smile when I see a response.

Kellan: I'm good. You?

Me: Same. Will you accompany me to Madeleine's wedding?

The infamous dots dance along the bottom of my screen for longer than I would like. The action could mean two things. He's looking for a way to let me down easy, or he's written a response, erased it, and tried again more than once. None of these bode well for me.

Kellan: Yes, but I have no intention of rekindling our relationship.

Well damn! Truthfully, sex with Kellan never fell short. Sadness grips me briefly. Then my choice to walk away floods back. I need to accept his terms this time.

Me: Understood.

I have a date and the promise of multiple orgasms coming my way for the wedding of the year. I haven't been with anyone other than him. Most men don't make it past a single date, and I don't do one-night stands. Then again, it's only been five months. Kellan is the exception to every rule.

We chat more over the next few weeks, firming our plans. No indication of starting over or trying again ever crept into our conversations.

The Wilton/Anderson wedding is held at a luxury hotel in the summer near the DC metro area. Madeleine and Christoph rented the entire hotel for their nuptials. The location is opulent and most importantly, private. The guest list is a who's who in the entertainment and sports industries. It was one of the few occasions I booked a room under my own name.

"Checking in. Demi Goldberg."

"Good afternoon. You're in room 4202. Your guest in 4204 joined us about thirty minutes ago."

I knew Kellan arrived because we shared our itineraries. The confirmation also helps me prepare to see him in person for the first time since breaking his heart. We have talked since then. However, the topics were civil. Nothing personal about us together was rehashed or discussed.

"Thank you," I reply.

"The bride and groom have set up in-room dining for this evening and breakfast tomorrow," the clerk informs me. "The cocktail hour begins at three p.m. sharp before the ceremony."

Sweet. No one will expect to see us until then.

The desk attendant adds, "The elevators are directly behind you."

I'm sure the staff was fully vetted given the star power on the guest list. I don't miss the twinkle of intrigue in his eye.

My nervousness increases as I approach the room. I'm terrified to lay eyes on Kellan again. This date is not us trying again. It's to have safe, sexy fun and not deal with outside pressure.

I inhale and hold my key to the electronic lock. Once it snicks open, I enter and wheel my luggage behind me.

"Kellan?"

He steps through the adjoining door and takes my breath away. He looks… hot as hell. In our time apart, he has packed pounds of muscle onto his already hard body. New team, DC, new training regime, it makes sense.

"Hi, Demi."

My heart falls a bit. Demi not Dolce.

The space between us might as well be the Grand Canyon. Despite the discomfort in my gut, I lean forward, brushing my lips across his, expecting him to pull away. Instead, he deepens our kiss. I'm likely setting myself up for a devastating heartbreak, but right now, I'm taking the risk either way.

When I open for him, he explores my mouth. As he withdraws his tongue, I follow, twisting mine with his. A primal look flashes in his eyes as he lifts my T-shirt overhead, revealing my bare breasts. He draws his hands down my back and hooks his thumbs in the waistband of my pants before peeling them down my thighs. After his fingertips graze the front of my legs, Kellan lifts my thigh, hooks it around his hip, and presses his unmistakable arousal against me. Grinding against him, I could make myself come easily. His shaft rubs against my nub in perfect rhythm.

"You need to stop if you want to reach the bed."

"Take me now. Right here," I command. I've never really seized control before. The power is a heady feeling when my words elicit a low growl. He pushes his pants and boxer briefs toward the floor and his erection springs free, grazing my soaked core. Turning, he sets my back against the wall before thrusting deep into me in one hard, breathtaking motion. Reaching between us, I circle my clit as Kellan pounds into me. The coils of a release tighten low in my belly. He reaches lower and lifts my other leg to his hip, opening me more. Setting my hands on his shoulders, I bear down, engulfing his shaft as he thrusts upward. I hold on to him tightly as he throbs inside me. As my inner walls constrict, I shudder around him, and he explodes.

Resting my forehead to his, I slowly catch my breath. Sex with Kellan has always been exceptional, but this time was somehow more despite his urging this is a fling. Slowly, he turns away from the wall, lowering me to the floor.

Damn! We never had an issue in the bedroom. It's been months since I've been with Kellan, and somehow, he makes my body respond and sing effortlessly.

I grab my clothes and step into the bathroom. He steps out of his pants and follows me.

I'm at a loss for acceptable topics to discuss. So I ask, "How is DC looking for next season?"

Kellan glances over at me puzzled while testing the water temperature in the shower. "That's what you want to know?"

"No, but I refuse to break my word to you."

He drops his head, strips off his clothes, then steps into my shower. His voice carries over the glass partition. "Honestly, we're looking good. It's possible with Preston and Jordan on the roster we could make a deep run into the playoffs."

"Good for you. The change in teams is promising?" I swallow hard. The reason he needed a new team was our breakup. The front office got wind of his retirement considerations and deemed him less than enthusiastic about the game and released him. The press caught Darius in a weak moment, and he shared the struggles Kellan was going through at the conclusion of the season.

"I guess so. What about you?"

"Filming and then promoting my films like before. I'm slated to work with Ellis again late this year."

"That's great, Demi."

Again with my given name. *Ugh!* Maybe this was a mistake of colossal proportions. The throbbing between my thighs indicates otherwise at least for my sex life. The last man to touch me intimately was Kellan.

Just a booty call with my ex. That's all this is. A pleasure-filled long weekend with a familiar partner. No strings attached. Problem is there are numerous threads, and they all run from my heart to his and back in a tangled mess.

He steps out of the shower and wraps up in a towel. He grabs his watch from the vanity and says, "Dinner will arrive in about thirty minutes."

I nod and step under the scalding water myself. After I shower, I tug on leggings and a tank to share a meal in companionable silence. I'm not sure what to ask or not, so I don't speak at all. I was expecting the amazing sex. I wasn't prepared for the disconnect between two people who are meant to be. Perhaps we missed our chance. The possibility that this fling could truly be the end of us is heartbreaking.

Kellan excuses himself to his room soon after we eat, and I don't see him again until he's dressed for the wedding. He knocks gently on the shared door.

"Come in, Kellan." I turn from the full-length mirror to stare at him. The man is hot in bold and all caps in sweats and a football tee. In a tuxedo tailored to his body, he's downright debonair.

His eyes travel ever so slowly from my toes upward. "You... would a compliment be weird?"

I shrug. "Maybe, but share it anyway. You look dashing."

"You're stunning. The emerald color is gorgeous on you."

My cheeks redden with his words. I know the mushy feelings and sweet words are short-lived, but it's nice to hear. "Thank you. Ready?"

He nods and offers me his arm. A battle rages in my heart and mind as I grip his bicep with my hand. This feels right. *No! This is temporary.* Two people with history and demanding professions taking a safe route. Not the best plan for my aching heart. I push my thoughts away, and we stride to the ballroom to mingle with the other wedding guests.

Soon after our arrival, Simon and Lucia, Madeleine's assistants, usher the guests into the atrium. The bride walks down the petal-strewn aisle.

At weddings, though I haven't attended many, when the crowd rises to watch the bride, I set my gaze on the groom. Christoph is attempting but failing to reel in his emotions. My gut pitches, and I drop my eyes to the floor. The only man I ever saw as my groom is beside me. Given the parameters of this date, the man won't be him waiting for me in a custom tuxedo at an altar in my lifetime.

"You okay?" Kellan whispers.

"Yup." I lie through my teeth. Either way, he buys my response or appears to. I compose myself and listen to the officiant speak about commitment and lasting love. With willpower I didn't think I possessed, I refrain from glancing at Kellan again until the happy couple breezes by us at the end of the ceremony.

The reception is fantastic. The guests from sports to movies and entertainment mingle and socialize after a delicious meal. Kellan and I even dance together. The R&B soundtrack has flickers of us playing on a loop in my mind.

"Nobody" by Keith Sweat leads to a suggestive few minutes of foreplay on the parquet floor.

Within ten minutes of the last bar of the song, we're fumbling with the key to our room.

Once the door closes us into my suite, he draws my lips to his. I'm momentarily shocked but dip my tongue into his open mouth. A moan escapes my lips as Kellan glides his hands along the length of my body and back up to cup my face.

After a light peck on the lips, Kellan turns me in his arms and draws the zipper as low as it will go. I turn and guide the straps down my arms and allow the fabric to fall into a pile on the floor. I'm standing before him in a white lace thong and sky-high heels. Given our history, I don't move to cover myself like I would with a new lover. I have his complete attention, and I'm going to enjoy it while it lasts.

Without a word, I tug on his bowtie and pull it from his neck. With painstaking precision, I open each button. His carved chest is on full display. I press my mouth to his skin and kiss a line to his waist before pushing his shirt and jacket to the floor.

Stepping forward, he drags his hands up either side of my curves. After reaching my shoulders, Kellan slides his arm around my waist and presses his body against mine.

"You're stunning," he whispers in my ear, eliciting a soft sigh.

"Thank you. You're pretty spectacular yourself."

He draws his tongue along the column of my neck and slowly walks us toward the bedroom. He gently sets me on the dressing bench and hovers over me before taking my taut nipple between his teeth. A sound of excitement and pleasure escapes my lips. I slide my hands down his sides, teasing the top of his boxer briefs. As he sucks my nipple into his mouth, I hook the waistband and draw them off his legs. Kellan sits back on his heels and lifts me to a seated position.

He pulls the lace thong off my legs and kisses upward, pausing at the apex of my thighs. My body tightens, as he rises. He presses my legs apart, licking from top to bottom repeatedly with urgency. It doesn't take long for me to squirm as ripples of pleasure roll in.

"Are you okay?"

Kellan draws circles with his tongue over my clit while slipping two fingers into my core. A soft moan echoes around us. As my release approaches, he speeds up the push and pull of his fingers. I tried to shrink away as the rush washes over me, but he holds me in place with a hand splayed across my tight abdomen. Kellan kissed his way up the left side of my body, stopping at the sensitive spot at my hip. Goose bumps erupt over my entire frame. It's a spot only he knows about. Kellan lowers his body on top of mine, his erection against my wet core.

"I want you," I murmur softly.

"Say that again," he demands.

Pushing as to why he needs to hear the words now is futile. "I want you," I repeat.

Kellan curls his arm around me, and we fall against the luxurious duvet. He positions the tip of his rock-hard shaft at my center before inching forward. Once he's fully seated, Kellan starts to move. My inner walls pulse around him. He thrusts forward and backward, and my release threatens sooner than I would have preferred.

I dig my fingers into his shoulder blades as the waves of bliss grow stronger.

"Yes, don't stop," I beg before my climax overtakes me. Shudders and aftershocks ricochet through me. He continues to bury himself in my center until he falls over the edge. Once our breathing regulates, we clean up and return to bed. Together.

I refuse to let the fact we're going to be over soon cloud what we just shared. The list of men with whom I have given myself completely is miniscule. It contains only one name—Kellan Oaks. I was a virgin when we got together. This fling was a massive mistake for my heart. Now I need to own it and piece myself back together without him.

CHAPTER FOURTEEN

DEMI

FEBRUARY 2022

The entire ride to the stadium, I go over my requests. I need complete privacy in the booth. I refused to be filmed, for starters. Kellan and I aren't a couple. Completely on me. My decision to step away from us was the hardest choice I've ever made. A sex-filled date at my agent's wedding led to another few weeks of debauchery.

Since our fling ended, I've hidden from the public eye and tried to forget. Kellan can make me quake with pleasure and shudder in bliss effortlessly. Nothing was off-limits when we were lounging, usually naked, in an over-water bungalow in Aruba.

The villa was private and luxurious. We defiled every surface and piece of furniture. For the first time in our relationship….

Containing a sigh is impossible.

We aren't nor ever will be a couple again. I need to own my reality. Kellan was my first and only partner. I trust him implicitly. I can be vulnerable and experiment. Toys, food, and unique positions were part of our getaway, including one called the pretzel and iron chef on the bungalow island.

"Miss Hepburn. We've arrived." The driver's voice breaks into my thoughts.

"Thank you." I exhale sharply and hope my privacy is protected. It's a lot to ask, but what good is my wealth without the ability to make outlandish requests? More importantly, I need to be here for Kellan's first Super Bowl appearance. I refuse to be a distraction for him.

A few stadium security personnel emerge with a large screen on wheels. I'm pleased. The elevator arrives on cue, and a second screen is waiting on the executive level. My request to be left alone was met with a spread of snacks and a private restroom.

I hesitate to stand near the glass overlooking the turf field. Then I recall my demand not to be filmed. I don't locate Kellan on the sideline until after a solid minute of searching. He's chatting with Jordan Devereaux and Preston Jameson. They are likely setting up the first few series of plays.

"Please rise, if you're able…," the public address announcer states. A young, up-and-coming country singer, Lauren Whitestone, stands proud and belts out the national anthem. If I recall correctly, she's a client of Valencia's. She is Madeleine's vice president at Scala.

It's been some time since I watched one of Kellan's games in person. Even then, I understood the privilege of luxury box seats. The atmosphere during a regular season game was fantastic, but the Super Bowl is off the charts. The fans are ecstatic, and my nerves cause flutters in my belly.

Am I entitled to be excited for him? Probably not. Would he acknowledge me if he saw me? I'm not sure.

I hold my breath as the ball is kicked off.

The silence around me is deafening. There isn't anyone shouting, "This is exciting!" to state my joy. Being here is exhilarating. However, I would've preferred it to be out in the open as Kellan's other half, not his high-profile ex. My feelings, not his, but still.

The opposing team runs the kickoff back to the thirty-yard line.

"Not too bad," I mumble to no one.

After a three and out, we have the ball at the forty. The DC team converted one first down before losing the ball on a fumble.

Kellan scrubs his hand along his face in frustration.

"Don't worry, the game just started," I say, willing him to hear me from afar.

I turn back to the field, my attention focused on Kellan on the sideline with a tablet in hand, talking to his teammate Cameron Beau. I know of him but never met him in person. The first quarter ends, and neither team has moved the ball much.

I wander over to the food spread and secure a drink. As I return to my seat, the roar of the crowd increases, and I focus on the game. DC player Tyson Beck intercepted a pass and ran it back for fifty yards.

Preston takes the next snap and hurls a pass on a slant route to Kellan. It's complete for twelve more yards. On the next play, Kellan runs a corner route along the far sideline. Preston releases mere seconds before he's tackled. He twists beneath the defender to see Kellan pluck the pass from the air and fall into the end zone. My former… everything scrambles to his feet and points to his heart before handing the ball back to the referee.

The rest of the second quarter passes without any additional scoring. Kellan and his teammates are up seven to zero at the half. During the halftime show, which I have no interest in, I use the restroom and fill my plate with food.

The third quarter starts out like the first until Preston connects with Cam in the end zone for a touchdown with nearly three minutes remaining. The crowd erupts in cheers. I throw my fist in the air and cheer for Kellan and his teammates.

The closer we get to the end of this game, the prouder I become. Kellan set a goal for himself, and he's fifteen football minutes from achieving it. No sooner do I turn my focus back to the field than Preston heaves a deep pass. Kellan is well covered by the opponent's safety. Not once this entire season have I seen him leap as high as he does to snatch the ball out of the air. I'm confident the smile on his face is from ear to ear. He lands near the edge of the field. The crowd waits with bated breath for the score to be reviewed. When the touchdown is confirmed, cheers erupt in the crowd, and Kellan points to his heart before trotting off the field.

I watch him walk to the sideline, except this time Kellan looks up in my direction. There's absolutely no way he knows I'm here. Even so, I take a few steps back from the glass to be sure.

Once he retreats to the bench, my gaze is pinned on him instead of the game. As the clock ticks down, elation courses through me. Once the time expires, I drop onto the cushioned seat and stare at the revelry below.

Confetti rains onto the players and coaches. Coach, Jordan, and Kellan receive a Gatorade shower.

Kellan walks onto the field and celebrates with Jordan, his better half, Alex, and his daughter Reese. Then Kellan jumps up and down with Cam and Ty. The entire time I study him with glee on his face, but my heart is in my throat. My chest aches, and I'm second-guessing this choice.

I yearn to break my own rules and rush the field to congratulate him on earning his first ring. Instead, I sulk as Kellan makes a snow angel in the fallen confetti near the thirty-yard line. When Kellan rises, he looks left and right as if someone called him.

He trots to the edge of the field and reaches up to hug his mama and shake hands with his older brother, Aidan.

I'm glad he isn't alone. I would prefer to be down there, but it's for the best. Kellan doesn't want me anymore. I hurt him deeply. Our fling was exactly that… a brief moment of wild behavior and enjoyment. The time we spent together can certainly be defined in that manner. I won't interfere with his life, nor will I attempt to be in the wings again. Not being all in hurts too much.

I watch the Lombardi trophy be passed around among the players as Jordan is announced the most valuable player of the game. Soon thereafter, the players leave the field for the locker room.

I reach out to the stadium staff and call for my driver. Within ten minutes, I'm in the nondescript sedan on my way to the airport bound for LA. I'm grateful for the ability and income to be here for this event. Sadness takes over. What if I'd tried harder to make us work?

CHAPTER FIFTEEN

DEMI

PRESENT DAY

It takes me a moment to find my bearings. For starters, I'm warm and cozy, and the blanket, if you will, is breathing steadily. I haven't slept as well as I did last night since… our fling. Sleep has always been elusive when I'm single.

I've dated… sort of. I've been out with actors, other athletes, and an accountant over the years. Not one made it past a second date. I compared them to Kellan down to their hand size. There's something about large hands that does it for me. Plus, his are calloused and beat-up from football.

I would be lying if I said I didn't search for Kellan and his new woman while we were apart. Page Six is usually on top of Hollywood and professional athlete dating lives. I never saw any indication of him moving on.

"What's on your mind, Dolce?" he mumbles against my bare shoulder.

I relax against him. "Us mostly. Well, how we got here anyway."

"Too heavy for first thing in the morning."

I turn and face him. Even with sleep in his eyes, he's the sexiest man I've ever seen. "I suppose it is. How did you sleep?"

"Amazing. Since we're doing this, I need to be honest, I wasn't sure how to handle you offering one of the guest rooms. I understood, but it felt—"

"Like a dismissal?"

"A little."

I close my eyes for a moment to gather my thoughts. Once I sort them, I meet his gaze. "I feel like slow was the way to go this time."

"Me too."

I slide my hand between us and cup his jaw. "Our relationship has been turbulent. Forgetting the bad periods would be detrimental to our future. However, waiting to experience the good times seems foolish."

"What are you saying?"

Leaning forward, I kiss him lightly and then push him to his back and straddle him.

"I don't care where you choose to play. If my vote matters, I think Arizona is the best fit for you careerwise. I want a life with you. It won't be easy, but it will be worth it."

"Every moment with you was worth it, even the lowest points. The minutes where my heart ached so much I didn't eat or bother getting out of bed. Recovering took intervention for me to move on."

"Darius?" I whisper.

He nods and continues, "When you chose you, it crushed me. I thought we were a team. It took me standing in the middle of a confetti-covered stadium… alone… to realize we were exceptional together and my demands were unreasonable."

I swallow hard and admit, “I was there.”

Kellan contracts his abs of steel, wraps an arm around me, and sits up. “Where?”

“At the Super Bowl, I saw you earn your ring.”

His voice cracks when he asks, “Why didn’t you tell me?”

“You were crystal clear after our fling. I couldn’t have more than just earth-shattering sex with you. I understood. I hurt you deeply. I stayed in the luxury suite until you left the field. I was adamant with stadium personnel my presence must be kept private. I’m still surprised the team accepted my terms.”

He cups my face with his hand. “I hoped you were watching somewhere in the world. I pointed to my heart after my two touchdowns.”

I remember those moments vividly. I inhale sharply. “Why?”

“For you.” His eyes close briefly before he adds, “I wouldn’t have that ring if I wasn’t traded after our breakup. The victory made me wonder if it was supposed to be that way. It’s one of the numerous reasons I’m here right now.”

“Please explain.” I guard my heart for the words he’s about to share. He won’t hurt me, but his sentiments might.

“I compare it to how I’ve seen every one of your films on opening weekend. In fact….” He kisses the tip of my nose and moves me back to the bed. He throws back the covers, crosses the room, and rifles through his bag.

Warmth and, dare I say, love bubbles in my chest. He has another frame for me. *Oh, Kellan.*

He takes a seat beside me on the bed and hands me the gift. "I have the ticket stub from every film. Now, you have a framed one for each of your Oscar-nominated pictures."

Tears well in my eyes, but I will them not to fall. "All of them? You don't…."

"I've viewed every project you ever created. You never cease to amaze me when you transform for a role. I don't love you as a brunette though."

I giggle softly.

"I do know what this gift means to you." We stare at each other for a few minutes before Kellan says, "Why don't we… I … make us some breakfast, and we can figure out our plan and where our last first date is going to be."

Elation passes through me, and I nearly knock him off the bed when I throw myself against him. I mumble against the curve of his neck. "Yes? We're doing this."

"Yeah, we are," he replies.

I refrain from spilling those three little words. While absolutely true, divulging my innermost thoughts is premature.

After a few steamy kisses, we leave the guest room and start our day. I grab a hoodie before I return to the kitchen. While Kellan pulls ingredients out of the fridge, I get started on the coffee. It's one thing I can handle on my own. My survival depends on it.

I set a cup near the cooktop for Kellan and take a seat at the island. "Offering to help would be foolish, right?"

Kellan laughs. "Yes."

Happily, I sit and watch him create a delicious and balanced dish with omelets, toast, berries, and a side of bacon. I'm not surprised Carol prepared for Kellan's arrival better than I ever could.

"Outside?" he suggests as he finishes our meal.

"Sure." I grab water bottles and shove them into my hoodie pocket. With our coffees in hand, I follow Kellan to the patio.

When we step outside, I inhale the crisp morning air.

"Is this typical winter weather?" Kellan asks before taking a bite of his food.

Today the temperature is in the upper fifties. Winter months on the West Coast are marked with cooler weather and rainfall. "The seasons kind of don't exist here, at least not the ones we love from the opposite coast. It certainly doesn't snow. Well, it's quite rare, usually a dusting at best."

A warm breeze cools us along with the birds chirping in the trees. I finish the food and find myself staring at Kellan. When I look at him, I see the guy I met all those years ago on the rooftop. So much has happened between us as a couple and separately as people. I'm waffling between overjoyed and terrified about our future. We've failed in the past. I refuse to succumb to the same fate this time.

"I can feel you thinking over there," Kellan states, meeting my gaze. "We can take on the world and win… together."

"Date first or calendar?" I ask.

"Both are happening this morning. Calendar."

I nod, grab my plate, and carry it to the kitchen. Kellan joins me and sets his dishes beside the sink. His arms curl around me from behind, and he rests his head on my shoulder. Instantly, I relax, and calm washes over me. No matter what was wrong, Kellan centered me. He was my peace and my safe space since I was a teenager. I'm looking forward to having him back in my life.

The water is running, but my range of motion is slightly limited. "If you let me finish this, we can get started."

He grumbles, kisses my cheek, and releases me. "Fine."

I laugh and finish loading the dishwasher as quickly as I can. "Come on." Threading my fingers in his, I lead him to my office. "Got a plan?"

His deep, husky laugh echoes around us. "Let's input the Arizona schedule and see where there are hiccups or areas of concern."

"You decided?"

He tugs me close and lifts me off the ground. "You were right. It's the best fit and a chance to win again."

"I'm crazy happy for you. What about the guys?" I ask softly.

"Let's find out." He pulls out his phone and sends a quick text.

We take a seat on the tufted couch and spread the sheets out in front of us.

"Ready?" I ask.

"Yes."

I grab a pen and add "Date night" to the calendar for tomorrow.

"Nice," Kellan states, and we continue forward. He glances at the pages. "Is there any reason you need to be in LA for the next few weeks?"

I purse my lips and wrinkle my brow. "The next thing I have is a fitting with Kelly. Then again, you have to be there too. I have to be available or go to her, wherever she is."

"What are the options?"

I smirk. "Look at us… communicating."

Kellan shakes his head.

I finish answering him. "Kelly's main boutique is in Maine. The other options are here or her home in Colorado. Why?"

"I want…."

"You can say it. We will get there eventually."

He takes my hand and kisses the top. "I want to go home and grab some essentials. I only packed for two weeks tops."

"I'll reach out to Kelly and see where I can fit into her schedule. Maybe we go to your place and then meet her." I cover his hands with mine. "Will you be my date?"

"Yes." His answer is slightly hesitant.

"I heard a but."

He turns to face me. "We need to consider every aspect, including security if we are going public then. Maybe our hard launch should be before."

"I agree. We don't need to hide, but we need to be smart about the reveal."

"Okay."

We move on and decide Kellan will join me on set for my film after the Oscars ceremony. Over the next two hours, we plan a vacation and a long weekend to Arizona to find a rental before training camp. Our schedule is complete for the next two years, including my work commitments and his as far out as the big game. We pause when we realize I would be filming during the Super Bowl. Hopefully, I can make it work. I would hate to miss the game.

His phone buzzes on the ottoman. Preston's name scrolls across the screen. Kellan reads the message.

"Preston is in. Now we're waiting on Jordan."

I barely refrain from breaking out in a happy dance. "That's good. What is the chance Jordan picks Colorado?"

"How do you…. Never mind. You're as good as any agent looking at the teams, and you read sports news like a fiend." He scrubs his hand down his face. "I'm not sure. He feels like Denver is a better choice for Alex and the kids. Personally, and perhaps a bit selfishly, I disagree. Of his choices, only Arizona is like DC as far as suburban living."

"I worked with Alex a few times before she left Blackthorne Security. She's awesome. If anyone can point out the flaws in Jordan's logic, it'll be her."

"Where shall we go for our first date?" Kellan asks.

I tap my index finger on my lips and reply, “Why don’t I plan one here, and you can set up one near your home?”

“I love that,” he replies. “Old school movie date tonight?”

“I’ll try to stay awake.”

Kellan laughs heartily. “Get planning, Dolce.”

“On it. You too.”

“Don’t you worry, gorgeous. I’ll be done after two calls.” Kellan laughs and checks his messages again. He wraps his arm around my waist and pushes to his feet, taking me with him. Kellan steps around the ottoman and turns us in a circle, shouting, “Jordan is in! Jordan is in!”

I giggle and pepper his mouth with kisses. “The trifecta together again will be amazing.”

“That’s the plan.”

Energy is zipping through him. I can feel him vibrating with excitement.

He kisses again with a bit more depth before asking, “Do you have a treadmill by chance? I need to run.”

“I do on the lower level. There’s a relatively flat three-mile trail in my backyard if you would prefer.”

“You have a route that long in your yard?”

I wrinkle my nose. “Not exactly. My property abuts a nature preserve. You can start the trail from the edge of my yard.”

“Blackthorne approved this house?”

I hear concern and worry in his question. "Yes. There are perimeter alarms on the boundary of my property for anything larger than a doe on two feet."

"If you can give me twenty minutes, I'll join you."

"You can plan a date that fast?"

I grin at him. "Didn't you do it in less time?"

"I will when I know the exact date."

My eye roll is epic. "Fine."

He kisses me and leaves the office. It's probably a good thing. His presence is distracting. I would rather strip off his clothes as a workout instead. I call my favorite Italian restaurant in LA and make a reservation for a private room tomorrow evening. Once set, I cross the hall to my bedroom to change.

I search for Kellan after tugging on leggings and a thin hoodie in bright colors.

When I find him, he's on the phone. He's dressed in athletic shorts and a fitted running tee. Instantly, my pulse increases, and my desire to lead him to bed returns. I nod and walk past him to the kitchen for bottled water.

"Yes. As soon as I have more details, I will share them. If you want to find a place out here, we can do that."

He must be talking to his mom.

"I already told Val to go ahead with Arizona."

He listens intently and then replies, "We are planning to come to the East Coast soon. Demi will be with me."

His mama speaks again.

He answers, “Without a doubt. Love you too.” Kellan hangs up and turns toward me. “Ready?”

“Yeah. Good call?”

My perceptive man tilts his head. “Yes. She’s happy for me professionally and personally. Mama never wished bad things for you.” Hope and gratitude wash over me. If anyone could hold a grudge, it would be Mama.

“I’m glad. She was nothing short of wonderful to me when we were together.”

“Well, you are going to get her back. She requested a dinner when we are at my place.” Nellie treated me as if I was her flesh and blood. I missed the support and love when Kellan and I were apart.

“I’m looking forward to it.”

He kisses my temple and replies, “Me too.”

I loop my arm through his and lead him out the back patio. Near the end of my property, I input my code and cross into the state park. Then I reset my alarm system. “When we get back, I’ll reach out to Jake and get you access in case you want to run on your own.”

“Thanks.” We stretch near the edge of the trail. “Are you running or walking?”

I scoff at him. “I still don’t run, Kellan. Go. I’ll be walking. You can cool down while I finish.”

He laughs, kisses me, and takes off. My pace could be described as a power walk like the old biddies in the malls. I soak in the sunshine despite its lack of heat and enjoy the fresh air. When I reach the nearly two-mile mark, Kellan slows to my pace beside me.

"Feel better?" I ask and hand him water.

"Not the reason for the run. I get antsy when my schedule is off."

"You don't take a training break at all?"

"Not fully."

I smile, and we finish our morning workout. This time together has been short, but I'm soaking up every minute. I believe him when he indicated this time was our last chance. I will do everything in my power to make it last the rest of my life, including sleeping on airplanes and being with him if only for a day. We're worth the effort.

CHAPTER SIXTEEN

KELLAN

Being in her private space is wonderful and uncomfortable at once. The awkwardness has dissipated somewhat since my arrival. For the first time in years, I'm looking forward to the future. Will our schedule hold up? All I can do is hope we accounted for every possibility. If not, then we will adjust.

Today was similar to yesterday. We had breakfast and then worked out. We stayed inside because of the rain. About an hour ago, she disappeared into her bedroom to get ready for our date. Demi requested I dress for a nice dinner out.

I opt for navy slacks with a crisp white Oxford shirt. To be honest, it's the nicest unworn outfit I have with me. With a spritz of Demi's favorite cologne, I wander into the living room to wait for my date. Ten minutes later, she steals my breath.

"You're gorgeous," I manage to say.

Her dress is midnight blue, off the shoulder, and cut to mid-thigh. She looks sexy as hell.

"Thank you. You clean up well yourself." A sly smile crosses her face. "Sticking to my favorite, huh?"

"Never stopped." I was wearing Bleu de Chanel the night we met. It was my choice for the premiere and for her since then.

"Ready to go?"

"Yes." I grit out. "If we don't get moving, I can't say we will leave your house."

Demi tugs her lower lip between her teeth, a move she is fully aware makes me hot and bothered.

"Can't have that." She extends a set of keys in my direction. "Let's go."

She has two cars in her garage, a luxury sedan and an SUV.

"You drive often?"

"Yeah. Never had an issue in the area. It's usually only big events where the public knows celebs will gather. We're going to enter the restaurant though the concealed garage entrance."

She inputs the address, and I follow the GPS to a nondescript concrete structure in the middle of LA.

I frown. "Are you sure?"

Demi giggles softly. "Yes. Stell and I come here when we have a girls' night out. No one bothers us."

I pull into a spot near a red door marked "Private", park, and round the vehicle to open her door. I'll relax once she's safely inside and tucked against me. In the early years of our relationship, we were discreet and never went out together. This is new and exciting. The bigger issue is her stardom and mine have skyrocketed since then. Do I want security with us on a date?

No. Will it be necessary once the paparazzi start seeking photos of us together? Probably.

"Good evening, Mr. Wolders and Miss Hepburn. Right this way." A tall, thin man wearing a black uniform guides us to the private dining area. To her credit, the only people who saw us enter were the kitchen staff. They didn't seemed fazed at all. Makes sense given we're in a high-end restaurant in Los Angeles.

We take our seats in the cozy space and check out the menu. Well, I do. Demi doesn't even open hers.

"You don't have to look?"

She smiles, and my heart skips a few beats. Her reaction is genuine and makes me believe we could pull off forever. "No, I get the same meal every single visit."

I glance down and finish reading. "The Caesar and the chicken parm?"

"I'm easy, huh?"

The urge to bite my tongue is strong. I don't. "Regarding food, yes. Other things, not so much." I cover her hand with mine and chance a look at her. I see my past, present, and future staring beside me again.

"Fair."

Perhaps our timing was wrong before. We've both been through tough patches together and apart. Maybe we needed to grow on our own before finally figuring out how to be a couple. Our server breezes in, shares the specials, and takes our drink and appetizer order.

Our drinks arrive, and we request the remaining items for dinner, including a special dessert requiring at least an hour of notice. I'm intrigued.

Demi raises her glass.

I follow suit.

"To us and our future together," she says with a slight hesitation in her voice.

"You have to trust me, Dolce."

Her eyes flutter closed briefly. "I'm not worried about you."

"I believe in us, and you will too. To us."

We clink our glasses together and enjoy a quiet dinner.

The meal is delicious, and the tiramisu is spot on. I escort her to the car, through the kitchen. If the staff figured out who Demi was, they didn't blink or call attention to their knowledge. When she sits in the passenger seat, her dress exposes most of her sexy, toned thighs. Before I close the door, she attempts to tug the fabric lower.

"Leave it," I plead.

Demi meets my stare and stops fussing with her dress. Delighted, I round the car and take my seat. Once I'm on the highway, I place my hand on her leg and draw circles with my fingers.

Goose bumps rise on her skin. The only sounds are the GPS and Demi's sensual murmurs from my fingers gliding over her soft, supple skin.

"Turn left. Your destination is on your right in six hundred feet."

About time. Touching Demi after so long has me rock-hard and ready to take her on the next horizontal surface.

We don't make it far into her house. I grip her hips with my hands and set her on the edge of the island. Demi immediately wraps her legs around me and hooks her ankles. Her dress hikes up to the point where I can see the color of her panties as well as the dark spot from her arousal. As she works the buttons of my shirt, I stare with hunger in my eyes.

"Are we sure about this?" I whisper.

Her hands pause at the bottom of the column, dangerously close to my erection. Her breathing is steady but faster than normal. Demi's eyes meet mine. "I…," she pauses to collect her words, "I've only been with you."

The weight of her words hit me square in the chest. "I haven't been with anyone." I wasn't a virgin when we met, but since Demi, it's always been her.

"I'm ready. You?"

I would like to say I hesitate, but I don't. I bracket her waist with my hands and lower her to the floor. With her wrists in one hand, I turn her away from me. I draw the zipper down her back and slide my hands down the length of her body along with the satin fabric.

"So sexy," I murmur against the top of her shoulder before returning her to the Carrara countertop.

The last time we were together, I took her against the wall of the hotel after tearing her shirt overhead. Today, my plan is slow exploration. It feels more intimate. Like before. Before the time apart, the breakup, the distance, and the pain.

I push the thought down and bite her taut nipple through the sheer fabric of her bra.

Demi shudders.

Deftly, I unfasten her bra and pull it away between us. She dips her hands beneath the collar of my shirt and pushes it down my arms. It pools behind me on the gleaming hardwood floor.

I palm both breasts and lower my mouth to her collarbone, then kiss along the valley between them before dragging my tongue along the underside of her breasts. Following her rib cage down to the dip of her waist, I press my mouth to a spot that makes her squirm. A spot only I know exists given her admission earlier.

Fumbling with the snap of my pants, Demi pops it open and draws my fly southward. She slips her hand into my boxer briefs and strokes me twice.

"Demi." I growl and hoist her into my arms. With a few long strides, I set her on the dressing bench at the foot of her bed.

She looks up at me as I gaze down at her. The hunger in her eyes is more palpable than I've ever seen before. Tearing my eyes away, I drag the side of her thong over her hip and press my mouth inside the curve of her hip, followed by a stroke of my tongue. Goose bumps rise on her skin.

"Kellan, again."

I comply and lower myself to the plush carpet before her. I slide my hands beneath her knees and pull her to the edge of the cushioned bench. Her blue eyes stare straight into mine. Starting at her toes, I kiss a path up her leg with excruciatingly slow precision to the inside of her left thigh.

Inch by inch, my mouth moves closer to her core. I drag the flat of my tongue from her pucker to her clit, followed immediately by my finger. Repeating this in reverse order a few times has her on the verge of splintering. The moment I spread her folds and spear her with my tongue, she convulses beneath me. I press a splayed hand on her lower belly to prevent her from wiggling away and missing out on the ripples of pleasure from my mouth.

"Let go, gorgeous."

The orgasm rips through her, the intensity harder this time. Before she has the chance to recover, I turn her away from me and place her feet on the floor. Immediately, I dip my fingers into her core and tease her nub. She's dripping with arousal as I withdraw my fingers, and I fill her from behind. Threading her fingers over mine, we rub her clit in a tantalizing rhythm. The rush of her imminent orgasm builds.

I thrust into Demi harder than ever before. Her inner walls tighten around me as her orgasm increases in intensity. My fingers dig into the flesh on her hip as my release mounts. Pleasure erupts between us, and I burst into her. Gently I withdraw and gather her against my chest before carrying her to the bathroom.

After a shared shower beneath scalding water, we turn in for the night.

When I imagined being with Demi again, our sexual escapades were never a concern. Renewed compatibility in the bedroom is an excellent sign of an amazing future together. Believing we're on the same page is the only way I can commit my whole heart again.

CHAPTER SEVENTEEN

DEMI

Late last night, we arrived in this picturesque coastal town in southern Maine. The chill in the air doesn't bother me as I overlook the waves crashing on the shore from our balcony. The salty air is soothing. Kelly assured me we wouldn't be bothered in this cute seaside gem, especially in the winter.

Kelly spent her summers here as a young girl. After college, she opened her boutique. Fast forward, she and Ellis fell in love and spend most of their time in the quaint area for stability for Nick and Ellie, their children.

I feel him approach before he says a word. Kellan's arms slide around my waist, and he draws me against his solid body.

"Morning, Dolce."

"Hi."

He takes a deep breath and says, "This place is something else. I've never been anywhere this peaceful except…."

"Aruba." I fill in the pause.

"That is one word for it."

I turn in his arms and ask, "How else would you describe it?"

"Torrid and sexy as fuck."

Heat washes over me from the memories flashing in my mind. As if he can read my thoughts, Kellan buries his face into the opening near the hood of my sweatshirt and presses his lips to my neck.

Blissful pressure rushes southward. “We can’t or we will be late.”

He groans and kisses my lips lightly. “Do I at least get coffee?”

I smile widely. “I’m so proud of your growth. Yes.” I turn and point up the street a bit. “See the white building? It has the best coffee around. I can’t come to York Beach without stopping at The Perk. Plus, it’s on the way to So Elegant.” If I recall correctly, the owner is Kelly’s sister-in-law or her bestie at least.

Kellan grumbles. “Fine. Let’s go and get this fitting business started.”

I laugh. “Your part is easy. Kelly or Billie will measure you and then you wait until I decide on my gown. Voila, the color scheme is done for you.”

He shrugs. “What am I to do in the meantime?”

“Sip your latte on the cushy couches in Kelly’s store,” I reply.

“Deal.” He kisses me again and disappears into our room.

Thirty minutes later, we’re walking hand in hand along the sidewalk toward our first hit of caffeine for the day.

The Perk is decorated with a *Friends* theme.

“Good morning. Can I interest you in a peppermint latte?” the young barista asks.

“Could we have a few minutes to view the options?” I reply.

“Sure. Take your time. Kelsey’s treats are all delicious.”

At the mention of her name, I ask, “Is she here this morning?”

The barista tilts her head. “Yes. May I give her a name?”

“Demi,” I answer without hesitation. I deduce quickly when people instantly recognize me when I’m out and about. The brunette behind the counter hasn’t put it together yet.

She nods and pushes through the double door behind the counter. Nearly immediately, Kelsey rushes out and hugs me. She’s gorgeous. Her and her husband met at Kelly’s brother’s wedding.

Adding space, she says, “It’s been a long time. How are you?” Before I can answer, she looks at Kellan and extends her hand to him. “Welcome to The Perk.”

“Kellan. Nice to meet you.”

Kelsey stares at me expectantly and with a look of “lucky girl” in her eyes. She should talk. I’ve met her gorgeous, overprotective husband. We’re both doing fine in the better half department. Over the years, I’ve wondered what longevity would be like with Kellan. Now, I’m holding onto him with both hands hoping like hell I don’t screw up again.

“You as well.”

Kelsey adds, “So? What are you doing here?”

I smirk and check to make sure we’re alone. “Kelly is dressing me for the Oscars.”

“Congrats on the nomination. That’s exciting.”

“Thank you. It is. I’m looking forward to it this time.”

The barista’s interest is piqued after hearing Oscars.

"Dolce, I know you want to catch up, but we can't be late," Kellan states pointedly while eyeing the clock.

"You're right."

He winks. "Say that again."

I laugh and place a large order, including lattes for Kelly and Billie. Kelsey and I continue chatting while our coffees are being prepared.

"Where did you find him?" Kelsey whispers.

"On a New York City rooftop, a long time ago. We've been trying to figure us out ever since."

"He looks at you like you hung the moon. I wish you the best. Finding a best friend of the opposite sex is the only way to go."

I wrinkle my nose and reply, "It really is a best-kept secret in relationships. Please say hello to William and the kids." She and her husband have two kids, Ben and Valentina.

"I will."

Kellan pays for our order, and we exit the charming spot loaded down with delicious treats, specifically a savory scone with cranberries and thyme.

"I hate to admit this, but this caramel latte is amazing."

I blow a kiss in his direction. "I tried to tell you. Kelsey never fails with her baked goods and coffee." We round the building and stand before the white door for So Elegant. I ring the bell.

Billie answers the door with a huge smile and a tiny baby in a carrier strapped to her chest. "Please come in. Demi, lovely to see you again. You must be Kellan. Nice to meet you." I'm not sure if this baby is her third or fourth child.

"I love the new space." The boutique has been updated since I was here last. Then again, my last visit was quite some time ago. The guest area is decorated in soft, neutral tones with white, tufted satin couches. The crystal chandelier remained though.

Kelly breezes into the lobby and greets us both. Kellan offers them the lattes we brought.

"Bless you," Billie states, accepting the cup.

He's silent for a moment, staring at the baby wistfully. Billie won't notice, but I do. Containing my sadness and grief is difficult. I manage to force my emotions away. The bliss of fatherhood he hasn't yet felt is completely on me as well.

"You're welcome."

I clear my throat to break the tension only Kellan and I are experiencing. "What have you got for me, Kelly?"

She grins and urges me toward the easels on the side of the room. She unveils a dreamy, dark teal column dress with sparkle on the hemline and bodice. The next option is an A-line dress in a soft mocha color. It's simple and would require jewelry to meet the pomp of the Oscars ceremony. The third option looks familiar.

"Is that…."

"A grown-up version of the first dress I ever created for you in deep violet. Yes."

"It's perfect!" I grab her hands and spin around in a circle with glee.

"I'm so excited to bring it back but better."

"What do you think, Kellan?" I turn and meet his gaze.

He composes himself before speaking. "It's beautiful. I appreciate the history with the design as well."

Inwardly, I frown. He isn't paying attention at all. Billie's baby is dredging up unresolved feelings. Rather than draw more attention to his response, I say, "Updated measurements, then?"

"Of course. Right this way," Kelly states.

I follow, and she makes notes of my bust, waist, and hips as well as the drop to the floor.

"Could you join us over here, Kellan?" Kelly asks.

His head twists abruptly in our direction. "Sure." He moves with the grace of a lion on the prowl to my side. I thread our fingers together. I'm not surprised to find his hands are clammy. "How can I help?"

"I need to see the potential height of her shoes compared to you. I don't want the dress to be too short," Kelly replies.

"Makes sense," he mumbles.

Kelly has me stand on a block about two inches high and measures again. "All set, Demi. Ready, Kellan?"

I watch as she jots his numbers down. My gaze is fixed on him. He's thrown by Billie's child. I knew fatherhood was a dream of his. Mine too, but I didn't realize how deeply the lost time affected him. It isn't something we can discuss right now, but we will later today.

"Where will you be a week before the ceremony?" Kelly's question draws my attention back into the room.

"My place by then. Right, Kellan?"

"Yes," he answers quickly.

Sensing the tension, Kelly replies, "Great. I will send the gown and tuxedo to your home a week before the event. You know the drill. Check it and make sure things are good."

"I will. Could you also send the items on my wish list?"

Kelly nods and makes a note. "It's great to see you in person."

"You too. Please give Ellis my best."

Kelly ushers Kellan toward the lobby and extends her hand to him. "Pleasure to meet you."

"You as well."

With a wave to Billie, we exit the store. Without asking, I lead him to the beach across the street. Despite the cold temperature, I take off my shoes and walk on the sand but Kellan doesn't.

"I'm sorry," I murmur while looking at the waves rolling in.

"Me too."

I wasn't expecting that response. For the first time, Kellan doesn't share the blame, as he shouldn't. I punted the possibility of carrying his child into the future. One we haven't discussed to be sure.

"I didn't…."

He nods and stares ahead instead of in my direction. "Today was the first time I've been around a newborn in years. I was…."

"Jealous." I fill in the blank.

"Green with deep envy like I've never felt before."

I step between him and the ocean while taking his hands in mine. "Motherhood is a construct for me, a figment of my imagination. I will be making it up as I go along. The only example I have is your mother, but I didn't meet her until I was a young adult. Truthfully, I only ever wanted to share a child with you."

"What are you saying?"

I hear a sliver of joy in his question. "I want to have your children."

His eyes close, and he adds, "Yeah… someday." His qualifier makes complete sense.

"When you truly believe I'm all in for us, you let me know. Then we can have a baby."

Joy, terror, and astonishment shine through his eyes. "Are you serious?"

"Absolutely."

"What about filming?"

"I'll figure it out. I don't want to put our family on hold any longer for my career," I reply plainly.

"How is that different from me retiring?" he mutters under his breath.

"Getting pregnant accidentally on purpose won't be the end of my career. Hanging up your helmet and shoulder pads is permanent usually anyway. My directors will just have to get creative with wardrobe and handbag placement. If Kerry Washington can carry a child while filming *Scandal*, I can pull it off too."

He curls his arm around me, lifts me off the cold sand, and spins us in a circle. "I want a family, but I also need to call you my wife. This chapter of our relationship is fresh and new. I trust you're in this, but it's only been a week. If I thought our history was enough, I would suggest eloping."

"I understand. My offer stands. I'm in. When you are on the same page as me, I'm ready."

"You aren't angry about giving me more time?"

I blame the tear rolling down my cheek on the cool ocean breeze. "No. I love you, and I will wait for you now like you did for me before."

Kellan leans forward and kisses me lightly. "Any reason for us to stay overnight?"

"No."

A twinkle appears in his eyes. If I had to guess what it means, he's ready to move forward by sharing his home with me.

"Want to go to Maryland now instead of in the morning?"

"Sure."

We scramble to our feet and walk to our room. We are wheels up within two hours.

CHAPTER EIGHTEEN

KELLAN

Waking with Demi tucked in my arms in my bed brings emotions swirling in my heart and mind. Even when we were apart, my soul knew Demi was my one and only love. Her offer to carry my child threw me a bit. I'm ecstatic we could be a family in a year rather than three or more, but pumping the brakes felt necessary.

We need to successfully navigate our schedules and stay together before I'm willing to bring a child into the mix, despite my desire to be a parent by now. I plan to be a father, not a baby daddy who sees his kid on a co-parenting schedule. We need to be on solid footing to support our goal.

"You're thinking awfully hard for first thing in the morning," Demi mutters.

I smile and kiss her head. "I'm not. I'm happy you're here. We have a date tonight and dinner with my family tomorrow."

She turns in my arms. "Mama?" Joy grows on her face.

"Mama, Aidan and his family, and possibly Micheline and her kids."

"Really?"

"Don't be nervous," I murmur and kiss her forehead.

Her smile widens. "I'm not."

"Yes, you are."

Demi draws her lips into a tight line like she does when she is carefully choosing her response. "Nervous may not be the right word. I trust without reservation you didn't trash me to your family despite the hurt I caused you."

I don't confirm her statement. More words don't seem necessary.

She continues, "I'm cautious, I guess. The last time I saw them or talked to any of them face-to-face was when Aidan showed up at my premiere."

I bolt to sitting and bring Demi with me. "He what?"

She bites her lips as if she said too much. "It wasn't a big deal."

Anger bubbles in my veins. "Tell me anyway."

Demi drops her gaze. "It was the first one after Mom died. You and I were restarting again slowly."

"I remember." I'm seething, and I don't know the full details.

Demi shares my oldest brother defended my honor and asked how she could break my heart again.

"Why didn't you tell me before now?" I mumble under my breath.

She cups my face with her soft hands, and I press into one. "Aidan didn't hurt me or Maia. He shared harsh words on your behalf. He was late to the party. I'm not surprised, since you normally talk things out with me, Mama, the trifecta, or Darius."

"Okay…."

"Please don't bring it up tomorrow. It was a blip, and he was trying to protect you from me."

"I don't like it, but I won't say anything unless he does."

"Fair. Willing to make me coffee and give me a tour?"

Before granting her request, I curl my arm around her waist and hover over her. "I missed this part of being yours."

"What? Deep heart-to-heart talks in bed?"

"No. Sort of. Right now, I mean waking up with you in a good place emotionally."

"Me too."

I lower my lips to hers and kiss her deeply. Do I care neither of us have brushed our teeth yet? Not at all. Am I worried about our date or dinner with my family? No.

My only concern is Demi and progress in being a couple again. Overall confidence is high for us on this final try.

A short while later, we get out of bed and start our day. With hot coffees, we walk through the house and settle on the couch in the master bedroom overlooking the backyard.

"It's peaceful here like in Malibu, but it's chilly."

"My closet is your closet, sweetheart."

Glee materializes on her face.

"You picked one earlier, didn't you?"

Demi sets down her cup, kisses my cheek, and hustles into the closet. Quickly she returns wearing a hoodie from my days in Seattle. We were good then. I'm taking it as a sign we can get back there if that timeframe is her choice.

"Still fits," she quips after tugging it overhead.

I'm sure she means my sweatshirt, but I hear her saying us and our life from back then is what she's looking for now.

I knock on the door of the bedroom. "Demi, our car is here." She kicked me out about twenty minutes ago.

"Coming."

Not yet. I shake my thoughts away and focus on my dinner date choice of attire. My jaw nearly hits the floor when she emerges wearing a slinky black dress molded to her curves. She turns slowly as she approaches me. There's a sheer panel between her breasts, and her back is completely exposed.

"You're hot as hell!"

"Thank you."

"You realize we aren't in California?"

She giggles. "Yes, I have a wrap by the door. Let's go."

I offer her my arm and escort her out the front door.

"Good evening, Mr. Oaks. Miss Goldberg," Jimmy, the driver, states, "Nice to see you both again."

I wait for Demi as she slides across the back seat. Then I sit behind the passenger.

"You know Jimmy?" I ask Demi.

"Yeah, he works with Scala frequently. How long is the ride?"

"Thirty minutes."

"Where are we going?" she asks. I'm honestly surprised she hasn't inquired long before now about the location of our date.

I take her hand in mine and kiss the back. "I let you plan in secret. Please allow me the same."

"Okay."

Tilting my head, I gaze at her momentarily shocked at her acquiescence. "Who are you? Where is Dolce?"

"I'm here attempting to make different choices than in the past."

My chest tightens. So far her words and actions match. I'm pleased. "Do you know what that means to me?"

Her eyes flutter closed briefly, and she replies in a whisper, "Yes."

We feel great now, but I'm skeptical for the times we need to be apart. The only thing I can do is trust in her and myself. This time will be different and better than the last.

Like Demi's choice in LA, Jimmy pulls down a narrow alley beside the upscale bistro.

At precisely 6:30 p.m., the side door opens, and the manager ushers us inside.

"Lovely to see you, Mr. Oaks. I have you and your guest set up in the private dining room upstairs."

"You as well. Thank you, Leon."

The bistro is decorated like a modern steak house with navy cushions and high-back chairs. A unique fireplace is central to the dining area. The vibe is cool and exclusive.

"This is gorgeous. How did you pick it?" Demi asks.

Leon laughs.

When I scowl at him, he clears his throat. "Enjoy your meal, sir."

I pull out her chair in the dining room. The décor is similar to the main area, but this is secluded and elegant.

"What was that about?"

"I'm a silent partner in this opulent establishment."

She smiles. "Good for you."

"Thanks. Initially, it wasn't performing well, but Chef Rivera is on the Michelin shortlist as of a few months ago. Metrics have greatly improved."

"How long have you been involved?" she asks as our server fills our water glasses.

We place our drink order and then I reply, "Three years or so."

"What made you invest here?"

"Chef is a great friend from college. I offered some startup capital in jest freshman year. She never thought her own restaurant would happen. I made good when I learned Annalisa was giving her dream a shot."

Demi peruses the menu while I stare unabashedly at her. "I can feel your eyes on me."

"Always, even when we were thousands of miles apart literally and figuratively."

"Sounds a little creepy."

I shake my head. "It's not any different than you checking up on me while we were apart."

"Fair enough."

We order our meal and talk about numerous topics, including a quiz on my family.

"Mama is healthy now?" Demi asks.

"Yeah, she has showed her hip who's boss."

Demi laughs, and our salad course arrives. I selected the Cobb salad while Demi chose a spring mix base. This meal isn't really about the food, although Annalisa makes every dish a championship event.

"I can't wait for a hug tomorrow."

Warmth cascades through me. "That's what you remember?"

"Of your mom? Her hugs are top of the list, but so many things. She was always kind and sympathetic to me."

"Mama knows you're important to me even when we aren't together. She asked about you and how you were."

"What did you tell her?" Demi covers my hand with hers.

"Honestly—"

"Yes," she interrupts.

"My responses depended on where we were in our relationship. When we were off, my updates were what I could glean from reports and stories about you. When we were on, I shared details about you personally, not Hollywood stardom. What about you?"

“I mostly confided in Carol or Estelle. Truthfully, when I returned home this time, Estelle called me out on my lack of presence.”

“Meaning?”

Our meals arrive before she can answer me. The fact Demi was ghosting everyone in her life gives some weight to the fact she doesn’t have time while she’s filming. Also, though, perhaps she should slow down a little. I won’t share my opinion with her yet. I understand her stance on the cyclical nature of the movie business.

Demi opted for short rib entrée, and I selected the lobster linguine. We dig into our meals.

“This is delicious. Annalisa has skills.”

I grin. “She does. What did Estelle mean?”

My woman sets down her fork. “She basically said when I’m on set, I ignore everything outside of my role, hoping said friend or boyfriend will still be there when I return. I happened to mention we hadn’t seen each other or spoken in four months. The reality was close to eleven. It made me realize I have to give a more concerted effort for my relationships while I’m working. It’s one of the reasons I feel the majority of the blame of our roller-coaster relationship is on me.”

“Did she reach out to you?”

“Yes.”

“We talked about blame. I understand your feelings, but I don’t agree completely. Estelle is on point though. The key difference is we didn’t communicate when we were apart.” I set my free hand over hers.

"I know, and our history will help me make necessary changes."

"I'm grateful to her for her honesty."

"I am too. Let's finish this food and eat dessert later."

My eyes widen. "I wasn't planning on bringing the flan home."

Demi lifts her shoulder and winks.

The ride home is short and sweet. Rather than pretend to watch a movie, we drop articles of clothing from the front door into the bedroom.

In the wee hours of the morning after twisting up my ultra-soft bedding twice, we gather our clothes. Sleep is necessary. Tomorrow is a big step forward. Seeing my family again as a couple.

CHAPTER NINETEEN

DEMI

My nerves are off the charts. Shortly, most of his immediate family will fill his home. I've met Mama, Aidan, and a few of his nieces and nephews over our inconsistent time together. For someone whose family is nonexistent for many factors, today is terrifying for me.

"You good?" Kellan asks, sticking his head into the bathroom.

My hands grip the granite countertop, and my gaze is pointed down. *No, I'm not okay.* "Yup."

He moves beside me and lifts my eyes to his with his hand under my chin. "Why are you scared?"

"What if they don't approve of me?"

He wraps his arms around me, safely tucking me into a cocoon of him. Kellan rests his head atop mine. "I love you. I want to be with you. They will see my happiness and support us."

Tilting my head up, I add, "I love you. I don't know how that looks or feels though."

"What?" His question laced with concern and preemptive angst on my behalf.

"Unconditional acceptance, not from family at least," I mumble and bury my head into his chest. "I promise you, this time is different. We've taken huge steps toward progress. I want today to be perfect."

Kellan laughs heartily. "You truly don't know how families work, especially large ones. Gatherings never go as planned, but we have fun and enjoy the company."

I take a deep inhale before chancing a glance at him again. All I see is love beaming down at me. I rise on my toes and kiss him lightly. "I can do this."

"We can." Kellan presses his lips to my forehead and releases me. "Come on, we have stuff to set up."

"Didn't you have the meal prepared?"

Kellan has a chef for him during the season. He also handles large family get-togethers as well.

Kellan grins. "I did, but we have other things to do."

For the next hour, we move tables, carry chairs, and decorate the tabletop. We barely finish before our guests begin to arrive.

With a tight hold on my hand, Kellan answers the door.

Nellie is a spitfire. She hands her son a bag and says, "Look at you! You're too skinny!" Mama calls me out and then hugs me close.

"Hi, Mama. The food at my last shoot wasn't great. I'm working on it."

"Good." She winks at me and then adds, "Hello, son."

He laughs. "Please come in, Mama."

"Don't mind if I do," she replies and takes a seat at the kitchen island.

"Would you like a drink?" I ask.

"Whatever you have is fine."

"Still prefer sweet tea?"

Mama grins at me. "You know it. Thank you for remembering."

I pause a moment to decide if sharing is a good plan, but I opt to say what's on my mind anyway. "Great people stick with you despite time and distance."

She nods and smiles at Kellan. Perhaps I should trust him. His words ring true at least pertaining to his mom.

"Demi, have a seat and catch me up. I believe congratulatory wishes are in order. The film was heartbreaking but wonderful at once."

I sit beside her, and we discuss about my award nomination. The Oscar is the big one of course, but others have come along as well, including Critic's Choice and Screen Actors Guild.

As we chat, more family members join the party. Mama introduces me but continues to talk with me.

"Thank you," I mumble.

"You're welcome, sweetie. A group like this is probably a lot for someone with a small, tight-knit inner circle."

She's on point. "I appreciate you more than you know."

"All I ask… please don't hurt Kellan again. He won't recover."

"Yes, ma'am. I intend to be here as long as he will have me."

Mama smiles and covers my hand with hers. "Very well. I only wanted my children to find a partner who makes them happy. I'm grateful you two found your way back to each other."

I lean forward, embrace her again, and whisper, "I won't let him down."

Kellan claps a few times, and the chatter in the house quiets. "Let's grab some drinks and then take a seat at the table."

Chef has been making trips to the table with platters of food. Honestly, there's enough to feed a fifty-three-man roster. There are two roasted turkeys, macaroni and cheese for the kids and teens, and lasagna with toasty garlic bread. I can only imagine the decadent desserts waiting in the wings.

Dishes are passed, and the conversation is casual and polite. Even Aidan has greeted me warmly. Looking back, I'm glad I didn't share with Kellan about the premiere. Earlier knowledge of the situation would've caused issues. Aidan was acting as the man of the family, as the oldest surviving son. Can't blame him for looking out for his brother. I will offer him the same assurances I gave to Mama. Then I will let my actions speak for me.

Between the dinner and dessert, the kids disappear into the basement. Kellan has a foosball table, billiards, and darts as well as a massive television.

As I clear some dishes, Aidan approaches, "Can I have a word?"

I nod and follow him to the far edge of the living room near the wood-burning fireplace. Kellan's home is beautiful. It's modern, cozy, and not fussy. The house is like mine except for location.

Aidan is a heavier version of Kellan. Their eyes are set the same, and he's equally as tall. Kellan has absolutely spent more time in a gym. Makes sense given Aidan is an architect.

He stares at me for a beat too long, making me rock back on my heels. I'm not afraid of Aidan. I wasn't even when he appeared at the premiere. I completely understand Maia's belief he was a threat though. I clear my throat.

"I'm not sure where to begin."

I acknowledge his statement and wait until he's ready. Like before, I'm not worried about my safety. To be fair, I did nothing wrong as it pertains to Aidan at all. He was acting on Kellan's behalf. I can't fault him for that.

"Over the years, I've hashed out this conversation in my head numerous times. It never turned out the same way twice." He drags his hand down his face as if not looking at me will matter. "I owe you an apology. I didn't have the facts. Seeing Kellan in such pain made me ill."

"You responded like a reasonable head of a family would. Maia was doing her job. I appreciate your sentiment. Your defense of Kellan's honor made me yearn for a family who would show up for me. My relationship with your brother is complex and complicated, but we are finally on the same page all these years later. I will never hurt him intentionally again."

"Thank you. He's happiest when you're beside him in life."

"I am too. With him, I mean."

Aidan smiles and adds, "What dessert do you think his chef prepared?"

I shrug. "Let's go find out." Turning on my heel, I walk back toward the kitchen. It appears he and Mama have been keenly watching my conversation with Aidan, likely to intervene if necessary. I'm grateful things are smooth now.

Every inch of the Carrara island is covered with delicious, sweet treats. I see cheesecake, chocolate cream pie, and an assortment of cookies to name a few of the options.

I join Kellan and slide my arms around his waist.

He leans in, kisses my temple, and asks, "All good?"

"Yes." I'm glad our conversation didn't devolve into a shouting match. I suppose time eases concerns and offers clarity. It also allows everyone to learn the facts of a situation before acting, which was an opportunity Aidan didn't have at the red carpet.

The kids rush upstairs and form a line at one end of the sugary row of goodness.

Maddie, the oldest niece, is first. "Uncle Kellan?"

He gives a nod of approval, and the kids converge with plates in hand without order.

The adults grin while they pick their desserts.

"Easy now! Grandma wants some too," Kellan's mother states.

Maddie turns and quips, "You know Chef has more in the pantry."

I look quickly and catch Kellan dropping his head as if he has been caught hiding the goods.

We laugh and devour the final course. Slowly, Kellan’s family leaves to travel home. I’m taking this meal as another step in our new chapter.

CHAPTER TWENTY

DEMI

I've been dreaming of this moment since I was nominated as a teenager. I've done as much preparation as I can. Blackthorne Security is in place and will accompany us along the red carpet, to the ceremony, and to the after-parties. My wardrobe is complete with a Kelly Barnett couture design and two other options for the post-ceremony soirees.

Kellan has been a gem for the last week. After family dinner, he boxed his clothes and some personal items. Luckily, we were able to fly them here with us. He has been patient and allowed me to vent when necessary. Kellan successfully kept me on task and reminded me I earned this accolade. I should enjoy it to the fullest. His words, not mine.

"When do we have to leave again?" he asks while checking his watch.

Bette and my glam crew are set to arrive any minute. I settle my nerves and reiterate the timeline.

"We need to leave here in three hours. Then we'll ride to the ceremony with Barrett and Marcello from Blackthorne." I have worked with both before, but not at once. They are imposing physically. Then again, so is Kellan. I was on the fence about having security at all. I realized this event will be our hard launch as a couple for good. I requested two bodyguards as a precaution. I don't anticipate any issues, but Kellan's move to Arizona is still in the news. He, Jordan, and Preston are signing new contracts together next week.

The doorbell chimes. "I'll get it." He kisses me and answers the door. After escorting them to me, Kellan disappears. Chances are, he'll go for a jog downstairs or outside. Despite the calendar set on March, the temperature is high enough for him to run the trail in the backyard.

After Lucia and Bette gawk over my dress, they get to work making me paparazzi and interview-ready. There are two distinct sides of me. The real me, who is comfortable in leggings and a ball cap for a late-night snack run. Public Demi takes primping and expert application of foundation and eye shadow. Even after more than a decade in this business, I can't achieve the same look as my glam team.

In the nick of time, the girls finish their work and help me into my dress.

"Oh my word!" Bette gushes. "Amazing!"

"You are gorgeous," Lucia adds.

I appreciate the compliments, but my insides are turning like a washer agitator. I'm dressed and ready for the Oscars. More important is our red-carpet appearance. I've yearned to have Kellan beside me, and today that dream will come true. "Thank you."

"We'll show ourselves out and send Kellan in," Bette states. We air hug, and they leave.

Standing before the full-length mirror, I study my reflection. This woman decked out in couture is ready to accept a golden statuette. Younger me wasn't. Teenage me didn't understand the gravity of the nomination itself. I do now. The accolade followed me to today. Oscar nominee. Now it's two-time nominee. At the end of today, I want Oscar winner on every future movie title. It isn't about ego. This film is epic, and the entire team deserves recognition, including Ellis. I look up and find Kellan standing behind me in the master. I'm not sure how long he's been there. He hasn't said a word. His expression is nothing short of mesmerized.

"Kellan?" I beg.

He steps forward but says nothing for a long while. Instead, he walks around me, slowly checking out every inch of my look. "You're incredible. It's one thing to watch on television, but another to be this close. I'm afraid to touch you."

"Don't be. I need you to settle my nerves."

Kellan smiles, leans forward, and skims his lips across mine. "Nothing to be worried about. Tonight is a celebration of your work. You deserve it."

Warmth, pride, and a bit of longing pass over me. This is what I've been missing. A person in my corner without reservation. Kellan is mine. I should've seen his unwavering support and love long ago.

He takes my hands in his and lifts them to his lips. "What do you say we go pick up your award?"

I nod imperceptibly. I refuse to believe I won until the golden award is in my hand. "Okay." Releasing his hands, I grab my clutch and slip my phone inside. "Are the guys here?"

"Yeah. They were about twenty minutes early. Marcello and Barrett make me feel small. No easy feat." Marcello Herrera joined Blackthorne

Security a few years ago. He's a former army combat veteran with an intelligence background. Barrett has a longer tenure. He's a former marine and single dad.

I laugh softly. "Let's go."

After a brief chat and reminders of protocol, for me anyway, the instructions are new to Kellan, we are whisked away to Los Angeles. The ride is uneventful. The guys are chatting about football and Kellan's move to Arizona.

Fine with me. My mind is busy. When they say no one prepares a speech, they're lying. I'm going over who to thank in my head for the entire ride.

As we pull to the back of the line, Barrett's phone chimes.

"Yeah, Jake."

I sit up straighter, and Kellan covers my hand.

"Breathe," he commands, and damn it, I comply.

"Understood. We will pull out of line and go for a short ride." Barrett ends the call and says a few things to Marcello.

I look at them expectantly.

Barrett clears his throat and shares, "There is a disturbance. A fan who is demanding to see you has been rushing each car as they approach."

Dread fills my chest. He wouldn't dare. I grit my teeth and tighten my hands into fists. "Who?"

Barrett and Marcello both glance at the other.

"Just tell me. I've had no security issues for years. Unless you and your firm haven't shared." My tone increases, as I expect a confirmation.

“If the threats were genuine, you would know about them,” Marcello answers.

“Meaning what? Someone calls Scala or Blackthorne, and you rebuff the inquiry?”

“Yes,” Barrett answers.

Ugh! “The day I intend to go public with my relationship and hoping to win an Oscar, everything goes sideways. Only one person in the world would dare.”

Barrett stares directly at me. “It’s your father.”

“What does he want?” I scowl.

Kellan immediately answers, “Do not entertain him, Dolce.”

Turning, I see anger etched on his face. “Is there another choice? I refuse to give up this walk for him. He has been absent for more than a decade. He wants to see me. Talk to me today. Why? There’s proof, I’m successful because I was nominated for an award.” I pinch the bridge of my nose and exhale slowly. “If I need to be in his presence when the show is over, I will.”

“I don’t like it,” Kellan states. His hand is threaded with mine, and his thumb glides over my skin. The motion is soothing.

“Me either,” Marcello admits.

I look at each of them directly. The air in the car is getting warmer by the second. It’s probably me heating up from this situation. “I will not budge. I have interviews and photo ops set up. I owe my fans.”

Barrett’s phone rings again. “Go ahead, Connor.” Connor is Jake’s partner at Blackthorne and his childhood best friend. He listens intently.

"Understood." After the call ends, he looks directly at me. "Event security has taken him into custody for breach of peace."

"Fine. Let's proceed to the line then," I state.

Marcello acknowledges me and informs the driver.

"Are you sure about this?" Kellan whispers.

"Yes. Stephen Goldberg is not ruining this for me. I have made something of myself without any assistance from him. Hell, he made success more difficult early on. I owe him nothing. He chose to leave me behind. Now he must live with it."

The driver pulls into the line, which wraps around the corner of the theater. We are about thirty minutes behind schedule. *Not bad.*

"Three cars ahead," Barrett states.

I check my makeup and inhale deeply before turning to Kellan. "Ready for this?"

"Sharing our relationship with the world? Yes. In this manner makes me a bit nervous though," he admits.

"Why didn't you tell me?"

Kellan kisses my temple and replies, "This isn't about me. I'll be fine."

"We're next," Barrett states.

The car stops at the beginning of the walkway. Barrett and Marcello exit, then Kellan. He extends his hand to me, and I stand between him and the car door. I smooth my dress and take a step forward.

This is it. Seconds later, with our hands linked, we approach the first spot. Photographers are clamoring for our attention.

"Demi! Who are you wearing?" A voice from the right shouts.

"Kelly Barnett Couture," I reply and glance up at Kellan. He's frozen stock-still. I turn so the cameras can't pick up my words. "Look at me." A solid minute later, his eyes meet mine. "Think of this as a post-game press conference after a big win. Smile and stare at the middle of the group. You with me?"

He nods and exhales slowly. The rest of the walk proceeds smoothly. We also participate in the E! News Glambot. The camera rotates to obtain a 360-degree image.

"Fantastic!" Kellan states.

I giggle and reply, "Yes, it was." Collectively, we sigh when we enter the theater. Inside, the pressure is much less. We make the rounds. I speak with some former co-stars and directors. I'm also a bit starstruck as Kate Winslet is nominated for her supporting role.

"Lovely to meet you," she states. Her gown hugs her curves perfectly.

"You as well."

"Your character development in the film was extraordinary. Good luck." She smiles and is guided to her seat. I barely contain my giddiness from meeting her when I find my seat. Thankfully, we're seated near Ellis and Kelly. I introduce everyone. Well, Ellis and Kellan haven't met. The lights flicker, and we take our seats.

I settle in for a long evening. Being on at these award shows is necessary. The camera could pan to me numerous times, especially as a nominee in a highly coveted category

During a commercial break about halfway through the broadcast, I use the ladies' room with my three shadows. Given my father's presence here earlier, the guys are being overly cautious.

"It's a lot, right?" the woman at the vanity asks.

I recognize her but can't immediately pull her name to the front of mind. "Yes, it is."

"Nice to meet you, Demi. I'm—"

Got it. "Pleasure is mine, Angelica." Angelica Swisher is also a Scala client.

"When they announce your category, take a few deep breaths, and smile, win or lose. Good luck."

"Thank you." I exit the restroom and find the guys chatting off to the right. I'm glad Kellan is more comfortable. While he has handled the press, before was for his professional life, not mine. Being arm candy is a new role for him. Thankfully he doesn't see the role as derogatory. "All set."

Kellan and I make our way back to our assigned seat. The fillers move as quickly as possible. For award shows, well-dressed young people fill the empty seats in case the camera crew pans that area. The producers don't want spaces during the broadcast.

"Dolce," Kellan says softly right before my category is about to be announced.

"Hmm?" I turn and see only pride on his face.

"Whatever happens, I'm crazy proud of you."

"Me too. I love you."

"I love you, Demi."

After a short speech, the presenter lists the names. I space out for a few seconds until I hear "...Goldberg in *The Woman in Black*." I recall Angelica's advice and smile, moderately but not widely.

The polite applause dies down. I thread my fingers into Kellan's and hold my breath. The blood in my ears deafens the sounds in the auditorium.

"And the Oscar goes to... Demi Goldberg."

Clapping erupts in the theater. I cover my mouth with my hands to hide the expletives that may fall from my lips. My chest feels tight. I'm on my feet with Kellan's assistance. I chance a look into his eyes. Tears threaten to fall. Regardless of the appearance of newness of our relationship, I kiss him and walk toward the stage.

I accept the statuette, which is heavier than I expected. "Thank you to the Academy for recognizing this film. Ellis's words were utter perfection. Bringing them to life was my honor. Thank you to Ellis Barnett, Madeleine Anderson, and the staff at Scala, and my glam team, including Bette and Lucia. Finally, and most important, thank you, Kellan, our road has been long, bumpy, and filled with potholes. Your faith in me is unwavering. I'm forever grateful." The commercial music begins. I blow a kiss to Kellan and walk backstage.

I have a few moments to collect myself with a glass of champagne before the photos and interviews.

Shortly after my first sip, Kellan with Marcello and Barrett beside him burst through the red curtain.

I don't even bother with decorum. I leap and throw my arms around his neck, knowing without a doubt, Kellan will catch me.

"I'm in shock!"

"You shouldn't be. You were born to play Elodie. Ellis's dialogue was superb, and you were recognized for delivering it as such."

His support never faltered even when we weren't a couple.

"What happens now?" he asks.

I laugh softly. "I take some photos, then some interviews, but I would prefer to get back out there in time for Best Picture." Our film is nominated in that category as well.

"I'm on it," Marcello offers.

I've been backstage for longer than I anticipated. Marcello returns quickly and escorts us to stage right for the announcement. I wait with bated breath more for Ellis than I did for myself.

"The Best Picture Oscar goes to *The Woman in Black.*"

We won! I jump up and down and kiss Kellan until Ellis makes his way to the stage. Joining him from the wings along with my other cast members is amazing.

"Congratulations," I share when I'm beside him.

"To you as well." His speech is short and to the point. The cast follows the same procedure I did after my win.

The rest of the evening is a blur. We attend the Governor's Ball and a few after-parties before returning to our suite. I collapse on the bed, still in my gorgeous dress with a wide grin. My cheeks hurt from smiling so much tonight.

Kellan flops down beside me after removing his jacket and tie. He hovers over me. “I can’t explain how proud I am of you. When you put your mind to something, you don’t fail.”

“Like us this time. I won’t falter. Thank you for giving me this chance. I love you.”

Kellan skims his lips across mine. “It’s as much for me as it is for you. I love you, Oscar winner, Demi Goldberg.”

I laugh, crane my neck, and press my mouth to his. After a few minutes of tongue twisting, we change for bed. Before I close my eyes, I chance a look at my phone. It is a mistake at least as far as supporting my emotional high. I hoped the issue with my father would simply go away, as he didn’t come into contact with me. More accurately, I wanted to ignore him completely. An email from Jake seems to indicate I may need to reevaluate my security in the future. Given it’s the wee hours of the morning and despite the fact I’m confident Jake would answer, I resolve to deal with my father later.

I refuse to allow him to derail my career again. I plan to block his second attempt anyway.

“Not good news?” Kellan asks.

“Jake. He’s worried about my father.” I climb into Kellan’s open arms and snuggle against him. Even with my father resurfacing, I’m safe and secure here.

"I agree with him. We will figure it out after some sleep."

I set my statuette on the nightstand. It's the last thing I see and will be the first when I wake. Perhaps then, I will believe today was real.

CHAPTER TWENTY-ONE

KELLAN

In the week since the Oscars, our life has included jetting to this interview or that photo shoot for Demi as well as a trip to Arizona for my contract signing with the DC trifecta. While we were in Phoenix, we met up with Darius to find a home. Ideally, we can select it from afar with his eye for our needs and security concerns.

We met with Blackthorne and decided to have a security check and upgrade at her home. We informed them of our intent to purchase a property near my new team. They will work with Darius as needed. Despite my urging and her security firm, Demi has opted not to have someone with her for this movie.

I don't love it. However, I agree with her. A security breach is virtually impossible for Stephen to show up on set. Crashing the biggest award show for movies knowing your daughter was a nominee is simple, at least knowing where Demi would be. Going forward, there would need to be a catastrophic failure of nearly every safeguard the film company, her agent, and Blackthorne put in place for her father to show up unannounced.

Now, we are waiting for her call time in her trailer. Demi has been up for two hours and checked off makeup and wardrobe. The movie is filming in Hollywood. Distance-wise, we aren't far from her house… our house. The reality is the film company requires her to stay in a hotel nearby rather than commute. Could she go home if necessary? Probably. Either way, I'm intrigued to see her work before it's audience ready.

A strong knock draws her attention. "Coming."

The frazzled woman with a headset says, "They will be ready for you in fifteen."

"Thanks. I'll be right over," Demi replies. The door latches, and she turns her attention to me. "Still interested in watching?"

"Hell yes!" My response is a bit more exuberant than it should be. While watching her work is fascinating, it's disjointed, repetitive and frankly boring.

She laughs. After grabbing her water and ensuring I have my backstage badge on, we head into the soundstage area. This is the first indoor scene she's filming. Since we've arrived, her schedule has changed three times. When Demi mentioned filming requires flexibility for weather and other inconveniences, she was on point. It seems each of the last four days, a new time sheet was slipped under her trailer door. Demi also doesn't have any leisure time. She is working from wakeup until her car brings her to the hotel. I never thought she was lying earlier in our relationship, but seeing it in real time solidifies her statement.

She's filming in the living area and kitchen of her character's home. In this movie, Demi is a single mother of a seven-year-old. Drawing on her own past will be helpful and possibly painful.

"Ready," Demi says to her on-screen child. Scottie is a young girl in her debut role. Her character's name is Morgan. Casting wise, the team did phenomenally. The actress is a small blonde, much like Demi was herself at the same age.

She runs downstairs and greets Demi in the kitchen. "Yes, Mama. Ready for school."

"Perfect. Let's go." Demi leads her daughter out the front door toward the neighborhood school.

"Cut!" A voice to my left shouts. From where I am, they stepped into a darkened hallway. I assume they filmed the outdoor parts earlier or will later.

A woman, if I had to guess, Scottie's mother, steps forward and guides her off to the sides. Demi walks over to the director and waits for playback. This happens four times before the producers move onto the next scheduled spot for the day.

I'm exhausted, and all I've done is sit here and watch. Boredom is a thing as well. For Demi to come to my "office" is different. Mine is a stadium full of people, joy, and fun. Those attributes happen once a week. She doesn't hang out when I'm training, in strategy meetings, or practice. It's something else for me to show up at hers. Hers is a movie theater in a year or more. My presence while she learns lines and repeats the same scene over and over until it's perfect is unnecessary.

Watching her is great, but I can't do this for any longer. Aside from the monotony, my exercise regime and nutrition are way off track. I haven't been able to adequately work out at the hotel gym. Plus, I'm exhausted from doing nothing each night when we return. It makes sense for me to go home, get back into my schedule, and visit her when she has time. As Demi mentioned with her eating on set while in Italy, the food sucks. I've lost weight since we've arrived. Not a great look for my upcoming training camp.

I completely understand why this only works because she's in the same state as me. Earlier in our relationship, she was in another country. Staying would've been necessary, more so when we are fortunate enough to have a family. The conversation isn't going to go well, but it needs to happen. The only difference between now and earlier in our relationship is Demi passing out beside me in the hotel each night.

A few hours later, the director shouts cut for the final time of the day.

Demi bounds over to me and takes my hand. "Ready?"

"Yup."

She tenses the instant the word leaves my mouth. I'm sure my sweaty palms and less enthusiasm is a sign. Plus, only Demi has been able to read me like an open book since day one. "What's wrong?"

"We need to talk."

Fear materializes in her eyes.

I add, "Everything is fine. We're fine."

She frowns and climbs into her car. I've been here since day one. I prepared her bag so she doesn't have to spend extra minutes in her trailer before leaving for the night.

Demi employs the silent treatment for the entire ride. *Great!* I thought we were being mature. She doesn't give one word until our suite door snicks closed behind us.

"Spill," she demands.

"Please take a beat."

My request is unheeded.

"Kellan, what is going on?"

I gather my thoughts. I don't need to. I've been thinking about this for at least a week. "I need to go home."

Her immediate reaction is heartwarming. "Is Mama okay?"

I shake my head. The fact she is worried makes my heart skip. "She's fine."

"I'm confused," she replies. "Let me get dinner." Demi crosses the room and orders food.

Pacing back and forth isn't helping me at all. I stop near the window and look out into the darkening sky. After ending the call, Demi stands beside me staring outside as well.

"Please explain," she mumbles.

My shoulders drop, and I turn to face her and take her hands in mine. "I love watching you work."

"But—" Her response short but not angry. *Maybe.*

"I can't stay on set. My training, nutrition, and sleep are jacked up. Losing more weight before camp is not an option." I lifted my gaze to hers to see her expression. Demi is excellent at her craft. I would bet two or three people can tell when she's genuine or acting. I am one of them. I expect more displeasure with my statement.

"I understand. Set life sucks most of the time. I wasn't lying when I said I had no free moments, and the food was terrible."

"I never said you were. Can I stay at your place?"

"Of course. We're in this together."

I mentally prepared myself for Demi to lose her mind. I'm grateful for her response and acceptance. I need to worry about my health and career for the season. "You aren't mad?"

Demi releases my hands, steps closer, and links her arms behind my back. With her head against my chest, she replies, "You've been here longer than I expected. I would appreciate more candor going forward."

"I wanted it to work out. My plan was to be with you as much as possible," I admit in the hopes of avoiding feeling like a failure in this stage of our relationship.

"I meant what I said. It isn't as if I can experience your daily work life. This gives you a better picture of how mine works," she states and looks up at me. "I don't want you to sacrifice your health or well-being for the extremely limited tangible time we get together. Frankly, sleeping beside you is wonderful as I missed it when we were apart, but we're truly getting an hour a day. We are typically eating and catching up on business matters. Well, I am. I get it, Kellan."

Shocked is the understatement of the year for this conversation. We have both matured when we were apart. The statement isn't meant as a slight to

Demi. The rigor of our professions is key to the dynamics we find ourselves in.

“Who are you and what have you done with my Dolce?”

My gorgeous woman adds space and grins at me. “I love that. Yours.”

“Me too. Truly, we are on the same page?”

She rises on her toes and kisses me lightly. “Yes. I will send a message to Carol. She will stock the fridge for you and probably ask for requests.”

A knock on the door interrupts our conversation.

“I’ll text it to you,” I reply before answering the door.

I set up our dinner, which includes two orders of baked chicken, veggies, and salad for me. Demi selected a cheeseburger tonight.

After her first few bites, she asks, “When are you leaving?”

“Tomorrow at midday probably. You have morning scenes, then a break before your night ones, right?”

She acknowledges me. “Yeah. I will arrange a car for you too.”

“I can handle a ride while you talk to Carol,” I state.

I was fully prepared to be uncomfortable with this conversation. I’m glad we can be adults about it this time around. I’m confident in our ability to be better communicators, that we will move forward together.

“After we eat, let’s plan when we can get together next,” I request.

She nods as I catch her mid-bite.

We use our time wisely once we finish our meal. Instead of going to sleep which we should, we tangle up the sheets until the wee hours of the morning. Being apart won’t be new for us, but being a couple with distance will be an adjustment. Demi is my best friend, and if anyone can figure out a relationship in our situation, it's us.

CHAPTER TWENTY-TWO

DEMI

Just two more days, two more days. I have been counting down until this film session is over. Early in our relationship, we weren't great at communicating. The times we were a couple but living separately were stressful and led to breakups often.

This chapter is much better. We have been talking daily either on the phone or video calls. Kellan has visited the set once a week since he moved home as well. Admittedly, the separation was lonely for both of us but necessary. Honesty is important. He initially stayed longer than I expected him to. Set life is boring and tedious especially when the director and crew are seeking perfection. They all do. Numerous takes are tough to watch for a non-actor who truly sees no difference between the first and final one.

The knock on my trailer pulls me out of my head.

Pushing the door open, I say, "Morning."

"They're ready for you," the production runner states.

Grabbing my water and a jacket, I close up and follow her to set. The remaining scenes are mostly me on my own. My character has been through the significant loss of her daughter. While I don't have a child, I have lost a close family member, and it wasn't pretty. Drawing on those memories and emotions will help me sell the grief despite the slight differences.

We are filming in an empty hospital room. Morgan is still in the bed, but she has already died.

"Action!" the director states.

"No! No. You're wrong. You said she would be fine. The surgery was successful."

Tristan Catchings, a charming, young actor, plays the role of the prodigy surgeon. "We did fix the issue in the operating room. She decomp—"

I'm overcome with shock and anger, shouting as loudly as I can. "She has a name. Say her name!"

The actor bristles briefly in reaction to me. It's on point and what is needed in the scene. This is the first film we've worked together. He clears his throat. "Morgan decompensated after we brought her back to her recovery. We resuscitated her. Once she was stable, we transported her to the ICU where the same occurred again. We were unable to save her life. I'm sorry for your loss." He turns on his heel and exits quickly and quietly.

At first, I freeze stock-still and stare at the monitor that once had her vital signs. The screen is black. I throw myself over my daughter's body and let out a bloodcurdling wail. I scream, calm down, and sob in a loop until the floor nurse appears in the doorway.

"We need to move your daughter, Miss." Kris has been wonderful since we arrived on the ambulance.

"I understand. What happens now?" My question is strangled with pain.

The nurse stands closer to me and holds my hands in hers. "We prepare Morgan for her final resting place."

I drop my head and stifle a heartbreaking wail. "Thank you."

"Of course," she replies. Kris waits until I gather my things and escorts me to the end of scene.

"Cut! Print. Perfect. No notes," she states.

I dry my eyes and inhale a few settling breaths.

An intern hands me some tissues and a bottled water. "Great job," she whispers. The stereotype of interns in this business is true. Don't be seen or heard unless spoken to. Well, actors believe the mantra.

"Thank you, Piper." I make a point to learn the names of the entire staff. I'm not a diva at all, and everyone deserves respect regardless of their role, from acting to directing to production.

"You're welcome," she mumbles and scurries away.

"Well done, Demi," Naomi states. She played the role of the nurse, Kris.

"Same to you."

The director waves me over to watch the playback. I'm grateful a second take is unnecessary. I'm wrung out after the first one.

Once the playback ends, the director calls for everyone to meet in the center of set. About ten minutes later with the cast and crew present, she states, "It was a pleasure working with Demi, Tristan, and the other actors on this film. Reshoots should be limited. A day early, we are a full wrap."

Cheers erupt around me, and I hug and wave to those who worked the film. With more pep than I normally possess, I rush to my trailer and finish stowing my personal items. Eager to get home, I packed most of my things last night. Did I know we were going to finish ahead of schedule? Not at all. Am I grateful? Absolutely.

Rather than tell Kellan, I opt to surprise him instead. I call the car service and request an early pickup.

"We have already been dispatched. Your car will arrive in fifteen minutes," the receptionist replies.

Damn! The production crew was fast. I'm ecstatic.

I start at the rear of my trailer and search high and low to make sure I didn't miss anything. Under the bed, in each cabinet and drawer, I verify the space is empty. Nothing. Confident I didn't leave anything behind, I wait for my ride home. The relief that I don't have to sleep alone in the hotel again tonight is palpable.

The loneliness of filming was different this time. I didn't close myself off to Kellan or avoid sharing my emotions. I put them out there for him, and he did the same for me. Before, I tempered the depth of my sharing to avoid conflict. This way is much better overall for both of us. I'm confident Kellan and I are on the same page this go around. Previously, we weren't.

The car pulls into my driveway slightly more than ninety minutes later. I hoist my bag to my shoulder and key open the front door.

"Kellan. I'm home."

He doesn't answer immediately. I drop my bag near the kitchen island and look around. Everything seems to be in place. In fact, my home is spotless. Before I freak myself out more, I check the garage.

Hmm. Only my car is parked in its spot. A ripple of sadness passes over me. He isn't home. I refuse to allow the past to spoil this. This is the first homecoming since we rekindled our relationship. Plus, I'm a day early. No way for Kellan to know. He isn't my mother. From the looks of the house, he was making sure it was clean for tomorrow.

Me: Hey! Where are you?

I grab my bag and start a load of laundry.

Kellan: On my way home. Why?

Me: I finished early. Hurry up.

His next text is a picture of the traffic ahead of him.

Kellan: As soon as possible.

Me: Does the promise of naked time help?

Kellan: Never a bad thing but can't move other cars.

Me: See you soon.

While I wait for him to arrive, I empty my purse and fall onto the bed. I don't lay there too long. Otherwise, sleep will overtake me. I haul myself to my feet, retrieve my bag, and empty my personal items into the master bath and office.

I hear the garage door open and rush toward him. Glee courses through me when he crosses the threshold. My inclination is to leap into his arms. It's been slightly more than a week since I've seen him. I pause when I notice his arms are full. Kellan is carrying a massive bouquet of my favorite flowers and a large bag from a high-end boutique in Los Angeles. Contentment bubbles in my heart and mind. He was preparing for my homecoming. Kellan of all people knows the impact of my mother's failures to make the transition easier earlier in my career.

Time passes as if he's setting the items on the island in slow motion. My foot is tapping on the floor. He probably thinks I'm annoyed. Anxious and excited are more accurate.

The longer the wait, the more active I become. Now, I'm jumping up and down. Kellan snatches me out of the air like one of Preston's passes and spins me around in a circle.

He peppers my mouth with kisses and holds me snug against his frame. This is the type of welcome I always wanted. Not the kisses, though the affection still rocks my world, but joy and happiness to see me after being away for work.

"I'm not done with my party setup," Kellan says against the curve of my neck.

"This is perfect. All I ever wanted was someone to greet me and a clean house. You've done that."

He pulls back and looks down at me. "I didn't though. You're early." The sadness in his eyes is almost too much to bear.

"You were setting things up. I love and appreciate you for making this return the best ever. We wrapped a day sooner than expected. I wanted to surprise you," I admit.

"As long as you're not angry."

"Not even a little." I rise on my toes and skim my lips across his. "Naked time, then pizza and a movie?"

"Yes and no."

I frown.

"Twisting up the sheets is happening before dinner. No pizza though, Carol made lasagna for me."

"I'm in." I step back and unzip my hoodie, revealing only a threadbare tank top beneath. There's no doubt he can see the outline of my hella expensive La Perla bra. "Did you ask her to teach you how to make it?"

Kellan wrinkles his nose and takes a step forward at the same time I move back. "I helped with this one actually."

"Uh-huh." I wiggle out of my leggings and toss them at Kellan before making a mad dash to the bedroom.

"Dolce!" Kellan shouts, chasing me. Within a minute, we're both sans-clothes between the sheets. Multiple orgasms later, for me at least, we share a long, relaxing shower.

While I dress, Kellan slides dinner into the oven.

I join him in the kitchen. Then I grab waters while he pulls out our dishes.

"How was your week of training?" I ask while we select a film to watch.

"Excellent. I had a video session with Billy, the team strength and conditioning coach, Preston, and Jordan. He made a few suggestions for me and added yoga for my quarterback. The grumbling from him was epic."

A professional athlete grousing would be my pleasure to witness. Hell, Preston would be the one to fall for his instructor.

Kellan responds, "Nah, Billy will select an old and ugly guy to ensure Preston does the work. Putting a hot, eligible woman in his vicinity would be a distraction we don't need."

I laugh so hard I nearly spit out my drink. "Preston is a player?"

Kellan shakes his head. "Not exactly. He isn't ready to settle down. So he opts for short-term relationships, mostly less than a year."

I nod and narrow the choices to *National Treasure* or *Ocean's Eleven.* "Pick your poison."

"Let's go with Nicolas Cage."

I select the movie and curl up on my couch. Kellan joins me and hauls me close. For us, friendship was never an issue. We are great in that arena. Now, progress is noted in staying together as a couple while leading fulfilling careers. For me there is still a quiet shred of doubt. Each day we remain steadfast makes the warning sound more like a whisper.

Before I push play, I ask, "Any progress with a home in Arizona?" Kellan agreed to handle the process with Darius. We are looking for a place to use during the season. If we need to upgrade or decide to relocate permanently, we will find a home with space and the amenities for the long term like a huge backyard and excellent schools.

"Darius sent over a few options. We can go over them tomorrow. Once we narrow it down, I can have Blackthorne do a security assessment."

"Perfect."

We start the movie and enjoy the first twenty minutes before a break to serve our dinner. Kellan and I watch both movies in the franchise before calling it a night. Climbing into bed with my man again is heavenly. I'm hopeful again for the first time we can actually pull off forever.

CHAPTER TWENTY-THREE

KELLAN

Since I signed my contract, I have been working with Darius to find a home near the stadium. Thankfully he's well-versed in the security concerns a professional athlete would have. In my case, Demi's stardom exceeds mine. Darius will come through for us. We don't need anything large, but most smaller places lack the privacy we seek.

Demi wrapped her most recent film a week ago. She has been catching up on her sleep and working her business before she needs to film again. We also selected two options for football season. I expect the security report from Jake today or tomorrow. We have three weeks before I plan to report for camp. While I intend to continue my pre-season training regime, Demi and I are returning to Aruba for a week where we stayed during our extended fling after Madeleine's wedding. Our flight leaves in a few hours. Near the end of training camp, she'll be across the country, ironically in Maryland. My house is close enough to the filming locations that the producers are allowing her to stay there instead of a hotel.

The resort was private and had stellar service. We plan to have some alone time before the season. On our way back, we will stop off and visit Mama for a few days as well.

"Kellan," she calls from inside her huge walk-in closet.

"Yes, Dolce?"

She's holding up two dresses, one fire-engine red and the other floral. I'm sure both are gorgeous on her curves. "You don't need either one. I don't plan on you wearing any clothes like our last trip to the island."

A fierce blush rises on her cheeks. She pauses before saying, "I'm fine with your plan. However, I need to be prepared if we do exit our villa."

I surround her with my arms and reply, "We aren't leaving, but go with the red. You look fine as hell in that one." Without a doubt, Demi will bring both. I will hold firm to my plans. We spent ten days in the over-water bungalow. This trip will be better because we are more than friends with benefits now. We're working toward forever, and I couldn't be happier or more excited to see where we go as a couple.

Hours later, we land on the tiny private airstrip. Within minutes, our concierge arrives and loads our luggage on the ATV.

"Good evening, Mr. Oaks and Miss Goldberg. Lovely to have you with us again. Per your request, we have you in the same villa as your last visit." The tall, thin man smiles. Whether he knows who we are or is genuinely happy to serve is difficult to ascertain.

"Thank you. We wish to not be disturbed. Please set our meals near the front door," I advise.

"Of course, sir," he replies then opens the villa and wheels our luggage inside. "If you require anything, please reach out. It's our pleasure to make your stay as perfect as possible."

"Thank you," Demi states, and he exits.

Rather than unpack, we both strip off our traveling clothes and hop into the shower. The walls are tiled from floor to ceiling, and one side is all glass facing the private beach. We clean up and dress for bed. Her pajamas indicate my woman has spent some money on sleepwear during her time away.

"New outfit?" I point from her nose to her toes. The set is a tiny tank top and booty shorts.

"You like?"

"Yes." No equivocation or waffling. She's gorgeous.

"We're resting tonight, right?"

"Dressed like that?" My words are strangled with lust.

"Let's not repeat before when we stayed up after our flight. It cost us precious sexy time."

I scowl and reply, "It did. Sleep it is." Climbing into the luxurious king-size bed, I can't help but curl my body around hers for the night.

The next morning, the sun peeks into the bedroom, warming my arm. Demi is still in dreamland, facing me with one arm under her pillow and the other draped over her waist. Her silky red camisole and matching shorts cover almost nothing, especially with the lace accents in appropriate—exposing her breasts—places. Resisting the urge to pull her nipple into my mouth is getting increasingly more difficult. Instead, I place a kiss on the top of her hand, the middle of her forearm, her upper arm, and the cap of her shoulder.

"I love waking up with you," she murmurs, her eyes still closed.

"Me too." Moving inward, I kiss along the lace edge of her camisole. Goose bumps erupt along her chest, and a soft moan falls from her lips. Her fingertips graze my chest in intoxicating lines. As I drag the thin silk strap down her arm, I latch onto her nipple.

"Kellan," she whispers, digging her polished fingernails into my skin.

I draw a circle around her nipple with my tongue while pinching the other one. In a quick movement, Demi pushes me to my back and straddles my hips. She's deceptively strong. Crossing her arms in front of her, she lifts the camisole over her head.

"Better?" She leans forward, offering herself to my mouth, her auburn tresses framing her flawless face. I prefer her natural starlight blonde to this color for her current film.

Instead of answering her with words, I bite on her nipple, making her shout my name. I feel her heat through her shorts and mine. Pressing her breasts together, I nip her other pink peak as she rocks against me. When I release her, Demi moves slowly down my chest, marking every few inches with her hot mouth. Licking my nipple with her tongue, she sends tingles along my spine. She travels below my rib cage to the point of my hip.

The closer she gets to my cock, the higher it jumps. Dipping her hands under the waistband of my shorts, she pulls them over my feet. Climbing up, she kisses a path along my leg and inner thigh. The warmth of her tongue touching my shaft has me arching off the bed. She licks upward toward the tip, circling it with her tongue. Holy fuck! As she teases the tip more, I focus on the blue of the sky to prolong these moments of pleasure. After taking me in her mouth, Demi sucks me deep. I can feel the back of her throat. I lean up onto my forearms to watch her beautiful mouth surrounding me. Each moment brings me closer to my release. Gripping under her arms, I pull her up.

"I wasn't done."

"I know." I'm not a patient man; when I want something, I go after it. I push her shorts and panties aside and swipe my fingers up her folds.

"You make me so wet," she murmurs as I bury myself in her core. With wide eyes, she meets me thrust for thrust. Gripping her hips, I lift as she bears down. No one has ever taken me so deep before. Her walls are tightening around my throbbing cock.

"Dolce, come with me."

Her hands fist the duvet around my rib cage. As I get closer, so does she. Her rhythm increases to match mine. As I explode inside her in short bursts, her body shudders with pleasure, and she plummets over the edge.

She lowers herself, plastering her perfect breasts against my chest, her mouth near the crook of my neck, her soft hair fanned over my arm. I've never felt this way before. There is only one explanation—her. Slowly regulating my breathing, I realize I'm so raptured with her I didn't use a condom.

"Dolce, I'm sorry." Panic zips through me. Then I recall our conversation in Maine. Still would've preferred to talk about it first.

"What's wrong?"

"I didn't use a condom."

"We. I'm just as much to blame as you are. I meant what I said, Kellan. If I get pregnant accidentally on purpose, whichever studio will have to deal with it."

I nod. "Do you need me to move?"

"Not yet."

She shakes her head against my neck, and I draw my hands up and down her back.

After a second round, we eat a late hearty breakfast and lounge around during the rainstorm. Trapped inside with Demi makes for a perfect day. Being anywhere with her is unmatched.

Our week was fantastic. The tenor was quite different from our first visit. During our fling, we defiled every surface we could find and probably invented a few new sexual positions. This visit was relaxed, calm, and about togetherness rather than only pleasure. However, we must return to the real world.

"Ready, Dolce?"

She frowns. "Can't we stay here?"

I laugh heartily. "Not an option. I will commit to a return trip within a year here or some other private tropical spot."

Her eyes light up. “Deal.”

Our concierge returns and escorts us to the airstrip. We board and take off for the East Coast. The flight is over four hours. Both Demi and I settle into our seats and nap. We went to my place after our flight and then to sleep.

Mama throws open her front door when we arrive.

She hugs Demi and greets her warmly. I’m grateful my mama and especially my brother Aidan allowed us to figure out our relationship on our timeline not some societal prescribed one. Our age difference is a key factor. We were on different paths that intersected randomly before.

“Hi, Mama. How are you?” I ask.

“I’m perfect. Two of my favorite people are here to visit. Plus, everyone will be joining us later.”

We step into her place and take a seat in the living room. She moved from my childhood home when I was traded to DC. This house is a cute Cape with three bedrooms. I thought it was too large initially, but the extra space allows for overnight guests.

“How was your vacation?” she asks. “You look rested, Demi.”

My woman’s face turns bright red. We certainly didn’t sleep while we were in Aruba after the first night.

“Our time away was exactly what we needed. With training camp up soon, Kellan will be working long hours. Then I have to film once more this year.”

“Where will you be?” Mama asks.

"East Coast actually. Well, we're filming in a mansion on the shoreline. It's set during the tourist season in a quaint seaside town."

"How lovely," she replies.

The judgment in my mother's tone isn't welcome. I briefly consider calling her on it, but I won't. Demi and I are in a great spot. We have a schedule, and it's working for us. Plus, retirement is still an option for me at the end of the season. The veterans say I will know when the time comes. I have at least this upcoming season in me. Beyond that, I'm not confident yet. The lull in the conversation has me offering assistance with the meal to avoid saying something inappropriate. "Can we help you in the kitchen?"

"Of course." She rises from the couch and leads us.

"You okay?" Demi whispers. "You went quiet."

"Yeah. Didn't like her response, but I'm not going to explain my choices to anyone other than you."

For the next hour, we assist in preparing a large family dinner, including pot roast, honey-glazed ham, and numerous sides, including Mama's award-winning macaroni and cheese.

My family arrives on time, and we take our seats at the table, which extends from the dining space into the living room. Perhaps I should've offered my house. Inwardly, I shake my head. We should be at Mama's.

Numerous conversations are going on around the table. Mine is with Aidan and the outlook for my new team.

My brother offers, "The three of you together again is intriguing."

"It's one of the main reasons I chose Phoenix. Regaining our chemistry shouldn't be too difficult. We were doing fine at our meet and greet actually."

Demi laughs with my sister, Micheline. It draws my attention and my brother's in that direction. The sound is one of my favorites in the world. I would admit hearing Demi share her feelings with me is tied at the top of the list.

"Happy for you both on the field and off," Aidan states.

"Me too. Thank you."

We bro hug and seek out Mama to help with the dishes.

"Uncle Kellan." My niece rushes into the kitchen.

"Yes?"

Wonder is plastered on her face. "Did you know Demi started in commercials and modeling like me?" Maddie is nearly six feet tall, and her skin is flawless. She's objectively beautiful. I'm not saying that because she's related to me. She has been in makeup and local clothing store advertisements.

I can't contain my laughter. "I did. How are the photoshoots?"

"Awesome. Mom said if I keep up with my team obligations and homework, I can take as many jobs as I want."

"Well done."

The kids and adults fill their plates, and silence befalls the house long enough for enjoying the first sweet bites. As I work on my half slice of cheesecake, my gaze lands on Demi. She's surrounded by the youngest

Oaks kids. Her patience is immeasurable as her dessert remains untouched while she helps with the wrappers or feeds them small portions.

I cross the room and join her on the floor. “Hey, want some help?”

“I’ll take it. Waiting to eat Mama’s chocolate ganache cake is a travesty.”

I laugh, lift my nephew into my lap, and assist him.

Demi savors the cake. Her reaction is just short of bliss, which I take offense to.

“Hey!” I lean closer and add in a whisper, “None of those noises here.”

“You might want to figure out how to bake this cake.”

I shake my head. “No need. I can make you moan without assistance from dessert.”

Her eyes widen, and I know it’s time for us to leave. As per usual, the goodbyes take nearly an hour from hugging everyone to Mama packing up leftovers. I don’t have the heart to mention most of it will end up in the trash.

“I will be there for the home opener,” Mama states.

“I already requested a box. Demi will be there, as will Darius,” I reply.

“Wonderful.” She hugs me and then Demi.

We leave and drive to my place until our flight first thing tomorrow morning. Our plan is to view two potential homes in Arizona before camp starts next week.

CHAPTER TWENTY-FOUR

DEMI

Kellan and I are set to visit two places approved by Blackthorne. The first option is a massive condominium near the stadium, which includes three bedrooms, a pool, as well as several levels of security, beginning with a doorman.

"What do you think?" I ask Kellan as he finishes checking out the third bedroom.

"It's fine. I'm not really picky where I lay my head at night as long as I'm beside you."

"Awwww! You're so sweet to me." I wrap my arms around his waist, and he kisses the top of my head.

"You don't like it?"

I shake my head. "It's different is all. I haven't lived in an apartment since I was a teenager." Interestingly, we both bought homes on our own, but they are quite similar as far as space and vibes.

"I get it. Let's go check out the second choice and figure out which we prefer."

We hop into our car and drive to the next option. The property is fully fenced and has a gated entrance. There are four bedrooms plus a casita. A casita is a small house, often used for guest space or an office away from the main house. The décor is closer to our style, but that isn't the main reason I prefer this home. It's warmer, less modern.

Kellan hasn't said a word. He's wandering around the house checking things out. I follow him in silence, taking in the amenities. The only thing this place doesn't have is a doorman.

"What do you think?" I ask as we step outside and walk toward the casita.

"You first," he replies.

"This one is perfect. It's bigger than we need though. There's space for Mama when she comes to your games nearby, but not in the main living area. She's not difficult—"

"I agree. She has been clear living with one of her children full-time is not on her dance card."

"Yeah, she has never minced words about her independence even during the early years of our relationship."

"Should I call Darius?"

I grin from ear to ear and bounce up and down like a child clamoring for candy. "Yes. Then we need to buy some furniture."

Kellan shakes his head. "We need to get the rest of our personal items here as well."

"True. Reach out. The rest will fall into place," I reply.

I wander slowly around the shell of a home. Elation passes through me. We just bought a home together. Most girls want a ring. The commitment was never our issue. Our problem was building a place for our relationship to grow and thrive. It seems we have three homes now, if you will, but either way we're in this together.

I find myself in the master bedroom and step into the double walk-in closet. Without a second thought, I lie on the ground to measure the space.

"There you are," Kellan says before bursting into a fit of laughter. "Why are you on the floor?"

"Measuring. All set?"

"Darius will send the paperwork to us and request a short-term lease if we can't get this closed in a week." A perk of the wealthy is to be able to make things happen faster than the norm. A cash purchase isn't unheard of in under a week.

"Perfect."

Apparently, my response wasn't satisfactory.

"What else is on your mind?" Kellan has always been able to read me clearly. Even on the rooftop, he saw the real Demi, and I love him for it.

"Nothing bad. I'm happy with our progress relationship-wise."

"Explain more," he states, drawing me into his arms.

While Kellan and I were apart, when we were dating but distance lay between us, I yearned for him to hold me. Without question, I'm safe and loved in the cocoon of him. "We… together—not you and I moved in or vice versa—agreed where to live as a couple. It was one of the aspects of our relationship that failed miserably before. I'm excited and proud of us for working on our future."

He exhales slowly before gazing down at me. "Me too. Straight to your place or food first?"

"Let's go back to LA and start packing. We can grab something on the way to the airport or order before we arrive at the house."

Kellan presses his lips to my forehead. "We just bought a house."

"We did." Joy cascades through my body. We are homeowners together.

"Come on. Moving boxes stand between us and our new normal. I love you."

"I love you."

The good news about our new home is the commute. While we're about thirty miles away from the stadium, traffic here pales in comparison to LA. Kellan drove a few different routes when we arrived, and none were longer than expected.

It's five in the morning on report day. Kellan is rustling around the closet. He'll be working sixteen-hour days for the duration of camp, which will last about a month.

"What can't you find?" I ask aloud.

He groans. "Sorry, Dolce. I was trying to be quiet to let you sleep."

I sit up and lean against the tufted headboard. I smile knowing we selected the furniture together. "No problem. What are you looking for?" I repeat.

"My Alabama undershirt with my name and number on the back. I wear it each year on day one."

I smile. "Does it have a frayed hem?"

He tilts his head as if I don't know the breadth of his wardrobe and what I can steal. "Yeah."

"It's in the third drawer on my side."

Kellan shakes his head and disappears. Shortly thereafter, he returns with his shirt. "I said you could wear anything. I meant it, but this tee needs loving care. Okay?"

"Deal."

He finishes dressing and sits beside me on the bed.

"Have a great day at work, sweetheart." My voice is syrupy sweet. It's nearly nauseating.

Kellan rolls his eyes and kisses me. "I'll be back late."

"Don't worry about me. Go kick some ass."

With another peck on the tip of my nose, he leaves the bedroom. I consider getting up to make him breakfast, but he prepared everything last night. Instead, I slide back under the covers.

I toss and turn for a few hours before giving up on more quality sleep. Padding to the kitchen, I find a single rose with a note that says "I love you." I lift it to my nose and inhale the scent.

When did he buy this? I shrug then pull down a highball glass to use as a bud vase. We certainly didn't buy one for this home. Kellan knows from experience, special gifts are important to me. I appreciate him remembering me on his first day. Before I overthink it, I send him a text even though he can't answer me.

Me: Thank you. I hope your first practice is fantastic!

With a freshly brewed cup, I curl up on our patio. It won't take long for me to hurry back inside. The temperature is scorching here in July under a huge umbrella near the pool. I'm a Big Apple girl who learned to love the West Coast. Overall, the location makes sense for international travel and, as evidenced by my filming this year, proximity to movie studios. The weather in our new home is an adjustment, but our relationship is worth it.

I retreat indoors before I finish my coffee as the sweat drips down to my brows. I decided to exercise before handling my business affairs.

We haven't lived here long, but our home gym includes a wall system. Each of us has a personalized program. I select a strength and stretching Pilates class and lower to the mat. I follow the instructions through the warmup, the hundred, cat, cow, boat, and even tree pose before I finish thirty minutes later.

I check my phone and find a reply from Kellan when I return to the kitchen.

Kellan: You're welcome. Excellent so far. Love you.

Me: Perfect. Love you.

With a smile on my face, I grab a small breakfast and scroll aimlessly while I eat. Then, I shower and dress for the day. First thing, I send an acceptance of a script to Madeleine. It would be the second installment of a thriller I did two years ago. Then I must finish reading two others. These films are set for late 2027 or early 2028. I will require the ability to work around a pregnancy if necessary, during contract negotiations. Have Kellan and I discussed a family again in detail? No, but I meant what I said. I'm ready to have a child whenever he is. We haven't stopped actively preventing a baby yet.

I settle into the oversized swivel chair in the corner of our shared office and flip open to the middle of the script. This film is a romantic comedy about a woman who needs to find a date before her grandmother's annual Valentine's Ball. The screenplay is witty and fun so far. The banter between the main female character—me—and my potential suitors is hilarious. I don't know how it ends yet, but I'm not keen on the proposed male lead, Rourke Talbot. He has a reputation for being a diva of epic portions on set. I don't have energy to go into a project with a hunch the days will be extra exhausting. Angelica Swisher has worked with him before and has declined every project that followed with Rourke. I trust her instincts. I've never worked with this director, but I have with the executive producer. If I love the project and want to do it, I may attempt to shift to a different actor.

My stomach grumbling forces me to check the time. I've been reading for a few hours. I push myself to my feet and prepare some lunch. Once I finish, I return to the office. I'm overdue to complete these read throughs. I finish the comedy, and I'm torn. The heroine ultimately chooses the man her grandmother suggested. He was her childhood neighbor as only fate could dictate. You know, the one who pulled her hair and made her mad at age eight. The ending is perfect. *Damn it!* I wanted to hate it so I wouldn't have to request a new co-star. *Ugh!* Instead of diving into the next one, I participate in some retail therapy before reheating Carol's lasagna. Technically, Kellan made it, but still.

I startled awake and see its dark outside. I fell asleep on the couch after dinner. Rather than wait here, I grab my second script and climb into bed to wait up for Kellan.

Near ten, he strolls into the bedroom. I expect him to be wiped, but he isn't. I'm sure he's tired, but he looks… rejuvenated as if this year, this team could be everything he hoped for.

"Hi. No regrets?" I ask.

"None. The rest of my teammates are amazing. The coaching staff is professional and prepared. This is my third organization, and it may be the best yet."

Warmth bubbles in my heart on his behalf. Kellan deserves a solid foundation at work as well as home. "I'm crazy happy for you and the guys."

"Move over. I need to grab some sleep. Back at it tomorrow."

I giggle and shift to my side of the bed rather than in the middle where there would be no room for Kellan.

With a quick kiss, he curls his arm around me and promptly falls into dreamland.

The entirely of camp is pretty much the same as the first day except for a few short trips for me to explore our new city. I found a cute boutique for clothes as well as a textile store for housewares. Normally, I would stay away from the latter, but I couldn't help myself when I saw the vase in the front window. The experience with this team seems to be going well for Kellan. He's more physically fit, well-versed on the playbook, and excited to open the season next week. This is the second instance we've been solid. The last time was in his rookie year, which seems forever ago. Perhaps this is an excellent sign that we are finally on the same page in all aspects of our lives.

CHAPTER TWENTY-FIVE

KELLAN

The urge to vomit has been present since the end of our walk-through yesterday. Not true, working out the details for the home opener has me on edge for the last week at least. I haven't been nauseous before a game since my rookie season. Intriguing that it was the last time Demi and I were on solid ground in our relationship as well.

She has been fantastic handling the details for Darius and his family, Mama, and Aidan. From security, securing a luxury box, flights and accommodations, Demi planned it all. I'm grateful and relieved, especially by her decision to have personal security for herself. Our hard launch at the Oscars went well. We haven't had any issues, but there are too many variables in a stadium in my opinion. If I recall correctly, Barrett and Lane will be with her today. I've only met Barrett, but Blackthorne has a stellar reputation, and their service is impeccable.

Mama and Aidan were not pleased with flying private, but Demi assured them it would be seamless and more comfortable. Commercial planes are fine and get you where you want to go, but you are beholden to their schedule. Pemberton will allow Mama and Aidan to travel late on Saturday and following a family dinner postgame on Sunday evening. On the other hand, they are happy to be staying in the casita rather than a hotel.

"Kellan." Demi sets her hand on my forearm.

"Hmm."

She frowns. "Are you okay?"

I cover her hand with mine. "I think so. I'm going over everything in my head, from the game plan to my locker room necessities."

"Deep breath, babe. Tell me what you have in your bag."

I list the contents from my game day undershirt from my rookie season, not to be confused with my camp tee, to my cleats. I'm not huge on superstitions per se, but wearing these two shirts throughout my career has kept me injury-free and on the turf. Who am I to question them?

"Headphones," Demi adds.

I rustle through the bag and don't find them.

"I'll check the car. Can you look in the bedroom?" I ask.

She weaves her fingers through mine, halting my search. "You won't be late. Why are you crazy nervous today?"

I relax with a deep exhale. "For the first time in too long, I feel as if everything in my life is in place. I'm afraid… I missed something big." Admitting this out loud is a huge step for me. Previously, I would've bottled up these feelings. Then again, I was usually alone when they hit.

"Oh, Kellan. You put in the work since you signed your new contract. Now you need to show the front office, your teammates, and most importantly, yourself you are ready for this stage of your career."

I lean down and kiss the top of her head. "You always know what to say."

A smile widens on her makeup-free face. "I try. Better?"

"Yes. Can you go check the bedroom?"

With her laugh echoing behind her, Demi hurries away to search for my noise-canceling headphones. At the same time, I scan the car. I locate them on the floorboard in the back seat. They must have fallen out of my bag.

"Found them."

She hurries back to my side. "Thank goodness." Demi wraps her arms around my waist. "I will be on the sideline with Mama and Aidan pre-game. After, we will meet you in the tunnel."

"See you there."

"Kellan, I'm thinking eighty yards and one touchdown should do for today."

I grin and pull a small notebook from my bag. Before each game as far back as high school, I scribble my goal stats. Demi is fully aware of this. This isn't my original notebook, because I filled one or two over the course of my career. I turned to today's entry and show it to her.

"One hundred twenty and one," she reads aloud. "The average works. Have a great game." Demi swats me on the butt, and I leave for the stadium. In addition to this ritual, my game day starts at least three hours before kickoff.

The drive is smooth and traffic-free. I imagine the same wouldn't be the case if I opted for one of the other teams.

"Morning, Mr. Oaks." Bobby the gate attendant greets me by name.

"Great day for a game."

"Yes, sir." He waves me through after checking my ID. Parking in the lot, I pull into a spot beside Jordan.

"Ready for this?" he asks after closing the tailgate of his blacked-out SUV. Side by side, we walk toward the player's entrance.

"Hell yes! We are going to start the season with a win. I heard Alex is sharing a box with Demi."

"Reese is so excited. I hope she doesn't drive Demi crazy."

Jordan's daughter may have lost her mind when she met Demi at family day during training camp. "I'm sure Demi's presence will be like the other celebs she's hung out with during your career."

"Possibly. Reese is a bit older now. She's fully aware your woman is a huge movie star and she gets to hang out with Demi during the game."

"Don't worry. Alex will be there, and our women will be fine. We need to worry about today's opponent."

Preston hustles to join us as we step inside. "Are we hyped?"

"Yeah!" I reply.

"I can't hear you," Preston states.

"Yeah!" Jordan and I shout at once.

"Better. Let's get a dub."

We burst into the locker room and prepare for the contest. Step by step, I follow my routine. It hasn't failed me yet. From my undershirt to putting my uniform on in a distinct order, I stay consistent. The stress of having my people in the stadium is newish. Mama and my siblings come to at least one game a year. However, it's usually mid-season.

I finish dressing for warmups and take to the turf. My focus is the game plan and getting my head right. Our preseason record was two wins and one loss. It isn't a great gauge of how well a team will perform over the course of season. If I recall the stat Coach offered yesterday, nineteen of the last twenty-five teams who had a .500 record or better went on to win the Super Bowl. The short answer is this team can win the big game, and I'm here for it.

Once I finish stretching and running routes with Preston and Jordan, I search the sideline for my family. I find Barrett and another tall man beside him. Barrett is the size of a mountain, and I'm not small in stature. A sense of ease washes over me. My family is safe and protected. Then I see Mama. She's talking animatedly to Demi about something on the jumbotron. I look up and find my initiative for bringing youth sports to the local community displayed. I started the program in my rookie year. For each team, I expand my reach to more young people. My foundation provides gear, tournament entry fees, and field rehabilitation as well.

I snag one more toss and chuck the ball back to Preston and motion to the sideline. Hustling to the edge of the turf, I stop at the roped area and hug my family.

"Thank you for coming, Mama," I say.

"No doubt about it. This is exciting. A new stadium and team. Well, some repeat teammates, I gather."

"Have you been studying?" I question her.

Mama, who chose a team shirt with my number on the back, laughs before replying, “Rubbish. Demi caught me up.”

“Of course she did.”

I bro hug Aidan and thank him as well.

“No place I would rather be. Of the teams you’ve played for, the vibes here are different in a good way.”

I nod. “I agree.”

“You look good out there,” my brother states.

“Thanks. Camp and preseason were great. I’m hoping the preparation leads to great regular games and a long playoff run.”

“From your lips,” Mama adds.

“I need to go.” I kiss Demi, nod to the Blackthorne guys, and hurry back to the locker room. When I reach the edge of the field, I realize Darius wasn’t with her. Nothing I can do now.

Thirty minutes later, the melody of the national anthem reverberates around the stadium. The trifecta huddles up before we line up for the first snap in red and white.

“Game one of twenty,” Preston states. The three of us bump fists and scamper onto the field after the kickoff. The first drive is rocky. Both Jordan and I drop a pass.

Only one I get today. I own the misstep and move onto the next play. We drive into field goal range and take the three points.

On the bench, I replay the drive and the mistakes we made. I realize the linebacker might have a tell, and I share the same with the guys.

"I'll look for it," Jordan states.

The roar of the crowd draws my attention to the field. One of our safeties intercepted the opposing quarterback. I tug on my helmet and hustle into the on-field huddle.

Four plays later, I break free on a slant route and leap to pluck Preston's pass out of the air and fall into the end zone. My first score of the season. I make a heart over the center of my chest while looking up toward the luxury suites. My eyesight isn't perfect, but I have no doubt Demi is copying the movement. I'm grateful my family let me figure out Demi was my person on my own. We had a small bump with Aidan, but otherwise I appreciate their support.

At halftime, we run into the locker room with a 24–3 lead. The offensive coordinator pulls the skill position players off to side.

"Gentlemen, you're killing it out there today. Execution is on point after the first series. Kellan and Jordan, keep it up. Follow the game plan, and we will secure our first victory of the season."

We put our hands in and listen to the head coach offer some insight before returning to the field.

The team struggles offensively in the third quarter. We drop passes and are stopped by the opposing defense three times. Jordan rallies the guys, and we score twice more in the fourth including a fifty-yard master class reception by Jordan. As the clock expires, I point up to the box and smile. Simply knowing she's here makes me happy. Pushing away the fact we'll be apart soon is necessary to live for today. We've learned from our past and will be better now.

After greeting the media, showering, and dressing, I greet everyone in the tunnel.

"Well done, Kellan," Mama says while hugging me close.

Aidan fist-bumps me from behind her.

"Thank you."

Darius shakes my hand next. "Sorry, we were late. Our flight was delayed."

I thread my fingers with Demi's. "No problem. Did Demi introduce you?"

"We're pals now," Mama states. "He is going to find me a luxury villa on the water in the Bahamas so I can retire in style."

I frown. "Are you serious?"

Mama laughs out loud. "Of course not. I love my little Cape."

Reese bounds over from her dad. Alex, carrying her son, Rowan, follows closely behind. "Can we go eat now?"

The adults laugh, and we make our way to the parking lot. Dinner is a great time. We catch up and share some stories. We shared a family-style Italian dinner and excellent wine. A car takes Mama and Aidan to the airport.

"I'm proud of you, Kellan," Demi says as we ride home.

I acknowledge her. "Thanks for pushing me to choose here instead of LA, which would've been easier for you."

"None are necessary. We're a team, small and mighty."

CHAPTER TWENTY-SIX

DEMI

We are five weeks into the new season. Kellan and his teammates are undefeated. I'm elated for them. I attended every game. Over the last two weeks, I have made a conscious decision to stay present with Kellan. Traveling for work is a necessity for both of us. I refuse to make the same mistakes from our past. I have set up a few surprises for him while I'm away.

"Dolce, I need to go," Kellan calls from the kitchen.

I inhale slowly and make my way to him. Separations were inevitable. Ideally, our history and gumption propel us forward this time. "All set?" I notice a box wrapped with a bow on the island.

Kellan drops his head. "As ready as I can be."

Sliding my arms around him, I stare into his eyes. "We can survive filming. Our plan is solid."

"I hear you in here." He points to his head. "My heart is still worried."

Lifting my eyes to his, I reply, "I am too. Our concerns and intentions will propel us forward when I return."

Kellan lifts my chin higher and kisses me as if he won't ever have the opportunity again. A deluge of warmth and love pumps through my veins. The force and passion behind this lip-lock ramps up my anxiety a bit. I suppose this is progress itself. Previously, I was completely oblivious to Kellan's emotional state before filming. With cautious optimism, I pull back and commit his expression to memory. I can describe every freckle, scar, and dimple in detail. He can as well for me. He exudes a little less confidence than me. I understand. The past was wholly my fault, despite him claiming half of the issues.

"I love you. I'll talk to you tonight," I say to urge him toward a timely arrival at work.

"I love you. Break a leg," he replies.

I laugh to the point of almost snorting. "Thanks." The well-wishes are typically for stage productions, but I'll happily accept.

He kisses my forehead and says, "Follow the instructions in the box, Dolce. No cheating."

"You too."

He frowns.

"You'll see, soon enough." I blow him a kiss as he leaves our home. The island serves as a support. The solid counter prevents me from crumpling to the ground with worry we can't pull this off. I manage to quell my tears and open the card on the gift.

Dolce,

Don't open until you land.

Love, KO

I'm intrigued but follow his request. I glance at the clock and speed up my exit from the house.

Less than thirty minutes later, I place my gift to Kellan on the island. As if on cue, Keith rings the doorbell.

"Good morning, Miss Goldberg."

"Hello." The driver grabs the handle of my bag and leads me to the car.

We arrive at the private terminal fifteen minutes ahead of schedule. As I've come to expect with Pemberton Airlines, the service is impeccable. Cash Morgan, the owner of the company, certainly knows how to cater to his clients. His status as a billionaire plays into the luxurious service as well.

To my surprise, Cash himself is my pilot today.

"Welcome aboard, Demi. Lovely to see you again," he states. "Congratulations on an epic award season earlier this year."

In addition to my personal Oscar and Best Picture. *The Woman in Black* also earned the same honors across the major award shows.

"Thank you. How are Noelle and the kids?" His wife is Ellis's sister. Cash and Noelle were held up with plane trouble on their way to Ellis and Kelly's wedding. Their meet-cute is straight out of a movie.

He grins from ear to ear. "Growing too fast for my liking, but wonderful nonetheless."

"Can't ask for much more."

"No, we can't." A spot deep in my heart aches. Pushing off having children has lingered in the back of my mind ever since I saw Kellan's reaction to Billie's newborn. My motives were both about my age and career, as well as rooted concerns that my upbringing didn't prepare me for motherhood. I walk down the narrow aisle and settle into my seat for a four-hour flight. Madeleine made sure I had plenty of reading material. She couriered two scripts for potential projects. It was most likely Simon, but either way, the package arrived late yesterday.

Midway through the flight, I take a break and check my messages and find nothing of note. My heart sinks momentarily, but then I recall he's at work and can't text me yet.

I bid Cash farewell and deplane. The transfer to Kellan's house is refreshingly short. I'm also pleased I can use his car to commute to set.

When I key open the front door, I'm greeted with a freshly cleaned house. I wander to the fridge and tug open the wide stainless door. My eyes feast on the fully stocked space. From prepared meals to snacks, my nutrition needs have been handled. He hears me.

Me: Thank you.

Mentally, I do time-zone math and determine he's in his afternoon meetings. I pinch the bridge of my nose and settle my nerves. We have a plan.

Once I calm myself, I pull my bag behind me, then set it on the dressing bench in the master bedroom. Unpacking goes quickly until I see the gift in my luggage. I pull the satin ribbon and reveal numerous envelopes. Without finesse, I tear into the one marked #1. Inside I find two puzzle pieces. I frown and then smile. He is going to make me work for this. Then I return to the kitchen. Within minutes, a well-balanced dinner warmed with a side of Diet Pepsi is ready to eat.

I curl up on the patio and admire the colors of early fall. Some of the leaves are beginning to turn shades of yellow and orange. I miss the stark demarcations of the seasons on the West Coast. With all the might I can muster, I fight the urge to allow old patterns to take over. Kellan isn't ignoring me. He's at work. Kellan isn't out with someone else; he's training for the game this weekend. My worries sound as if I don't trust him. I do… completely. My own insecurities and stunted sense of family is completely on me. Instead of spiraling, I change hastily and walk on the treadmill in his home gym to clear my mind.

It's been months since my father disrupted the red carpet at the Oscars. With Madeleine and Jake's assistance, I was able to avoid appearing in court. I submitted an affidavit of facts for the judge. I didn't bother to check on the disposition. He hasn't made another attempt to speak to or see me since.

I stop the belt when Kellan's gorgeous face appears on my phone.

"Hey, baby. You're welcome."

"How was training?"

He tilts his head, trying to piece together where I am. "Why are you in the gym?"

"Walking off some tension. I'm good."

"You sure?"

I exhale slowly. "Yes. Leaving for this movie was difficult. The last time, you were with me." Calling the property home is a massive transition for Kellan and me. Our relationship was less about the structure and more about the feelings and desires between us. For the first time, I truly believe we're on the same page.

"Then I left."

"I know. Coming to the set was more to show you my day. Honestly, I didn't consider the impact on your fitness and nutrition. It made sense for you to return to your schedule then. That reason also follows why I'm alone at work now." I shake my head and add, "I'll be fine once the director screams 'Action' tomorrow. Right now, I'm alone in one of our homes. I miss you already."

"Same here, sweetheart."

We chat about the game plan for this week's game.

"Make sure you text me your stats," I request.

Kellan grins. "I will. Thank you for the gifts." I left a mid-size box on the island. There are a wide range of gifts from puzzle books to novels to cheesy little trinkets. The purpose is to keep our relationship front and center while we're apart.

"Welcome. What do the pieces make?" My gift has numbered envelopes. The first one contains two puzzle pieces. Of course, they are opposite corners.

He shrugs. "You will have to wait a bit to find out. Talk to you tomorrow."

I end the call and shower. Then I wiggle beneath the covers. It's earlier than normal, but the reasons for turning in now are twofold. First, it'll speed up the time until filming starts and hopefully the desperate loneliness will decrease. Second, sleeping in this huge bed won't be easy. When we're together, I'm usually plastered to Kellan's side all night long.

The blaring alarm startles me awake. I fight the rush of sadness. I'm alone and throw back the covers. I only gave myself a short time to get out of the house. Every bit of sleep is welcome during shooting.

The ride to the set near the shore was traffic-free due to the time and season. Filming scenes for a summer beach movie in the fall makes sense as far as cinematography. It gives the cast and crew nearly complete control of the surroundings.

I'm greeted by a showrunner. "Good morning, Miss Goldberg."

"Kimmy, right?"

The tall brunette nods. It's clear she hasn't worked with me before. Knowing the names of the cast and crew is important for a production to run smoothly. I make it a point to learn them from day one.

"Please, call me Demi."

"Right this way, Miss… Demi." It isn't as if Kimmy didn't listen, but she's not used to such latitude in this business.

The trailer is standard, and I drop my bag on the table in the kitchenette.

Kimmy states, "Wardrobe is three spots to the left. Hair and makeup is five. The director requests we begin with the outdoor beach scenes starting with the meet-cute in two hours."

"Thank you. I'll head over now."

She turns on her heel and scurries away. If I had to guess, this is her first film in the role. Kimmy seems terrified to mess up. My character doesn't have a lot of hair and makeup, considering it's set on a beach in the summer. I avoided tan lines, especially when we were in Aruba.

A flash of our time in the tropical paradise bubbles to the surface. I smile and push it away. Now is a great moment to be recalling how soft Kellan's lips feel on my…. As pleasant as the memory is, I need to focus.

Normally, first days on set are rough. Everyone is trying to figure out boundaries and navigate unforeseen issues. This film has started well. I only hope the trend continues for the duration of the movie.

CHAPTER TWENTY-SEVEN

DEMI

Nearly three-quarters of this shooting schedule has passed. Kellan and I have done well communicating and sharing our feelings this time. No more wallowing in sorrow or loneliness. We went back to the first days of our relationship and use video chats as long as possible daily. His team is doing well, having only lost twice so far this season. A playoff run is likely. The thought reminds me to reach out to Ellis and keep him updated as I will be working with him during the post-season.

Each day I open an envelope and reveal at least one piece. The puzzle appears to be a photo of us from the NFL draft many years ago, but I still have a bunch to add.

Me: Have a great game. Send your stats. Love you.

After messaging him, I leave for set. The weekends are not days off when you have permits, leases, and shooting deadlines. The good news is today is only intended to be four hours long. I should be back home to watch Kellan's game.

Once I arrive, we jump right into today's work. I'm not surprised. Everyone is eager for the afternoon off. We knock out the first scene in only four takes.

With the director pleased, the cast and crew set up for the second spot earlier than anticipated. This scene is on the outdoor patio of the set house. It needs to be filmed during the morning hours for timing in the script.

"No, you can't do this to me now!" I shout at my co-star.

"I have no choice. You have three weeks to move out or I'll evict you."

I summon tears and reply, "This is my home. Don't do this!"

"You left me no choice, Leah." He delivers his line and storms down the beach.

We do three takes.

"Cut!" the director shouts. "Playback check."

As I walk over, Kimmy flags me down. "Your phone has been vibrating incessantly from the same person."

"Who?"

"Aidan Oaks," she answers.

Oh no! I snatch my phone from the table beside her and listen to my messages.

"I'm in Arizona for Kellan's game. Oh, crap! He's fine. It's Mama. She's on her way to the hospital. You're the closest family member. Can you get to her?"

I exhale. Kellan is fine, but I instantly worry about Mama. If I had thought about it more, I would know the game hasn't started yet. Fate is on my side when the director ends filming for today.

I press redial while I run to my trailer for my personal items.

"Demi. Thank you!" Aidan says when he picks up.

"I need more info."

Aidan relays the details.

"I'm driving toward Mama."

Driving at a high rate of speed on unfamiliar roads is not my favorite thing to do. I'm grateful to be nearby enough to be present for Mama. Never once did she make me feel as if I was the problem. She welcomed me with open arms even when I hurt Kellan deeply.

When I arrive at the hospital, I screech into a parking spot and rush headlong inside. My hands are tingling from gripping the steering wheel tightly. I didn't consider my attire or who I am nor my lack of security. Kellan would have my neck under normal circumstances. My goal is for Mama not to be alone.

I slow at the reception desk. "Can you direct me to Nellie Oaks? She was brought in by ambulance less than an hour ago."

"Your name, ma'am?"

"Audrey Oaks." It's a play on the alias I use at hotels and Kellan's last name. Mama will understand, assuming she's conscious. Aidan didn't have any details other than she was injured and being transported here.

The young man picks up the phone, presumably to find out the correct location to send me.

My head is toward the ground as much as possible. My stardom is usually a blessing. I would prefer to keep a low profile today.

He taps the keyboard, and a visitor pass rolls from the printer. "Take this. Follow the signs for the emergency department. Mrs. Oaks is in room four."

"Thank you." I hustle away and follow his instructions to the letter. When I reach Mama's room, I'm taken aback.

Her head is bandaged, along with her right arm. She appears to be sleeping. The monitor displays her vitals, which appear correct despite my lack of medical training. I pull the chair closer to the bed and take Mama's left hand in mine. She doesn't stir. Renewed concern ripples through me again.

I consider waiting but call Aidan despite not having much information for him.

"How is she?" he answers.

I fill him in on what I'm seeing. "No one has been in since I arrived. I will let you know more when I do."

"Okay. We are deciding when to fly there."

"I'm here. Kellan should play in the game."

Aidan huffs. "I'm trying to get the point across."

Aidan and I agree on something. "Good luck. He's a tough one when it comes to Mama."

"I understand."

"Not in a bad way," I add to temper my words.

"Demi, we're good. I'll do my best." Aidan's response is candid. He's being honest. His hill is steeper than mine. Considering Kellan came running for me when my mother was dying, I have no doubt he will want to do the same for his. There's a stark difference between my drug addict, alcoholic mother and Mama. The latter has the will to live and see her family thrive. Mama's disposition allows Kellan time to work in my opinion.

I ended the call and watch her heart rate line run across the screen. After waiting for nearly an hour, a young, chipper, raven-haired nurse steps into the room. Her name tag bears the name Cass.

"Oh. And you are?"

"Her daughter-in-law." Not exactly true, but it will be eventually. "Can you update me?"

"Of course, but has anyone told you, you have an uncanny resemblance to an actress?"

"No, afraid not. What happened?" My intent is to push the conversation away from me. The last thing I need is entertainment news programs to find me here. True, our relationship is widely known, but Mama doesn't need additional stress.

"She has been in and out of consciousness and hasn't shared any details regarding her fall."

"How do you—"

She cuts me off by adding more. "The first responders found her at the bottom of her rear steps. Her neighbor called for assistance. We are unsure how long she was outside before the request for assistance was made."

"I understand. I see her injuries are bandaged. Have you run any tests?"

The nurse reviews Mama's chart. "I see a request for imaging of her head and arm. Waiting on transportation."

"Thank you."

Mama is taken away about twenty minutes later. She's gone for a short time. Then the clock-watching begins again.

I rest my head on her hand and fall asleep. Her hand tugging from beneath me wakes me.

"Where am I?"

Swiping the cobwebs from my eyes, I rise and talk to her. "You're at a local hospital. What happened, Mama?"

She frowns. "Is Kellan okay?"

"Absolutely. I'm here for work and closer than the rest of the family."

Her body sinks in relief. "The last thing I recall is hanging some clothes out on the line. Now, I'm here."

Her clothesline is set on the corner of her back porch, which is off the second-story kitchen, if I recall correctly. Maybe she lost her balance and fell while trying to secure a pin. I won't suggest those details as the truth, but that story is possible. "Okay. Why don't you press the button for your nurse? They will want to know you're awake."

She complies and lifts her right hand and wrinkles her nose in confusion.

"Trying to remember?" I ask.

"Yes, but it may be futile."

Cass appears in the doorway. "Nice to see you're awake. Can you tell me what happened?" She then proceeds to check her vitals while Mama shares the same scenario she did with me. It isn't much to go on though.

"Thank you. Your vitals have been stable since your arrival. We're waiting on the results of your scans." Cass leaves the room.

Mama nods and then retreats into her head. Her arms are crossed over her chest as best she can. She's flustered at not knowing what happened. Mama would hate it, but perhaps she needs to move into the casita permanently. Inwardly, I shake my head. Not my place. Plus, we're never home. I could stay with her while I'm filming when she's released, but then what?

"Can you turn on the game?" Her question draws my attention back into the room.

"Sure." I hope he stayed. This matchup is against a division rival. More importantly, Mama expects to see him on the screen.

With bated breath, I wait for the commercial break to end. The defense is on the field now. It's nearly halftime. The score is tied at ten. I attempt to utilize telepathy with a cameraman I've never met. I'm willing him to pan to the sideline.

As the clock expires, I spot Kellan running into the tunnel and relax. Aidan must have been uber persuasive.

Minutes later, my phone is ringing.

"How is she, Dolce?" Kellan's voice is raspy and laced with worry. If I didn't know he was in the locker room, on the verge of tears would be more accurate to convey the anguish in his voice.

"Talk to her." I extend my phone in her direction. "It's Kellan."

I can't make out his words, but I overhear, "You should be listening to your coach."

Kellan obviously replies.

Cass steps into the room with a doctor.

Mama continues, “Rubbish. I don’t recall what happened, but Audrey is with me. Go score a touchdown or two, then fly here. The Oaks women have this covered.”

Kellan says something else, and Mama offers the phone toward me. “The doctor is here. I’ll keep you posted and book you and Aidan a flight. Love you.” I turn my attention to the physician.

“How are you feeling?” the doctor asks.

“I’m fine. My arm is a bit sore, but otherwise good.”

She pulls a penlight from her white coat and checks Mama’s eyes. “No headache, dizziness, or nausea?”

“No.” Her answer is short and sweet. I hear the plea to get her home hours ago as if this isn’t necessary fuss.

“Your scans are clear. You don’t have a concussion or other head injury. Your forearm has a hairline fracture though. Nurse Cass will provide you with a hard splint. It needs to be worn for at least six weeks. A repeat X-ray will be required to verify healing.”

“Thank you, doctor,” I reply, and she leaves the room.

Mama looks up at the screen. The second half has started. Kellan snagged a high pass from Preston and scampered into the end zone.

“Woohoo!” Mama shouts.

“Big fan?” Cass asks.

“He’s my son.”

My stomach bottoms out, and Cass stares directly at me. My lie is now exposed.

"I'm here for her. The last thing anyone needs is a swarm of unwanted attention on your emergency room. Please discharge my mother-in-law and we'll be on our way."

Cass replies, "Of course. I'll expedite the paperwork."

"Thank you." Once she leaves, I handle a flight here for Kellan and Aidan. I update Aidan with the details. I also make a note to ask Simon to send a swag basket to Cass.

"Great. We will be back as soon as possible," he replies.

"I got her."

"I know. My earlier doubts were unfounded. I'm sorry."

"No need to apologize." Aidan's concerns were reasonable at the time.

"I spoke with my wife and sister. They will be reaching out."

"Okay. See you later." I end the call and assist Mama with her clothes as much as she'll allow.

"I can do it." She's adamant until she tries to lift her arm overhead.

"May I?" I whisper as if the volume of my request will soften the blow of requiring assistance.

She closes her eyes and drops her head in agreement. Once her shirt is fixed, Mama says, "I don't want my children to worry about me. I can take care of myself."

I hold her uninjured hand in mine. "Maybe it's time for a little help."

"I refuse to be a burden." She scowls.

"You never could be, Mama. Let's get you home."

Cass returns with the discharge instructions. "If you want to pull a vehicle to the emergency entrance, I'll bring Mrs. Oaks to you."

"Go," Mama shoos me away. I navigate to the game on my phone and give it to her.

A wide smile grows on her face. I hurry to the parking lot and pull the car around.

Cass assists Mama into the front seat.

"I greatly appreciate your discretion."

She looks left and right. No one else is around. I checked. Twice. "Your performance was epic. It was a pleasure to meet you, Audrey."

"You as well." I round the vehicle and pull away.

"She figured us out, huh?" Mama asks.

"Yeah. It's okay. We are on our way with no press. Remind me of your address, please?"

She replies and returns her attention to the game.

I input the details into the GPS and ask, "How's it going over there?"

She smiles again before I pull away from the curb. "Kellan scored again. He has three now and one hundred seventy-six yards. They are up by fourteen with five minutes remaining."

"Perfect."

I escort her inside and have her take a seat in her chair. I set a pillow on the arm.

Handing her the television remote, I ask. "Tea?"

"Yes, thank you."

Mama's kitchen is set up perfectly. The kettle is on the stove, and the tea is stocked to the right of the cups and saucers. When I finish preparing the beverage, I find her sound asleep.

I check my messages before searching for a task to complete to assist Mama.

Kellan: We'll be there by eight.

Kellan: There aren't enough words to express how grateful I am to you.

Me: None are necessary. We show up. I love you.

Kellan: See you soon. I love you.

Truth is… Mama never failed Kellan and me. She supported us from afar and never passed judgment on me for my shortcomings in life and love. Her advice was stellar. Mama knew Kellan and I were soulmates long before we figured it out.

The house is spotless aside from the laundry she hung out earlier. I glance at the staircase for a clue as to what happened but come up empty. An accident? Perhaps Mama lost her balance. Either way, she's going to be fine eventually. I pull in the clothes, fold them, and place them on the chair in her bedroom.

As I'm leaving the master bedroom, I notice the photos on the sideboard. Each frame has a joyful moment for her family. They appear to be in birth order. I walk to the end to see an older picture of Kellan. My heart seizes, and tears well in my eyes. This woman exemplifies a true mother. The final frame has an image of Kellan and me from the Oscars red carpet. Perhaps with Mama as an example I could pull off motherhood. While I promised Kellan babies, my doubts about being a mother are as deep as the Mariana trench. Then again, no one knows what they're doing until they are in the throes.

A few hours and a late dinner pass before Kellan and Aidan burst through Mama's front door.

"You came?" Her question is shaky.

"Of course, Mama," Kellan replies.

"Demi took excellent care of me and fended off a nosy nurse."

Kellan's eyebrow rises in question. I wave off his silent inquiry.

Aidan hugs her while Kellan crosses the room to me. He hauls me into his arms and holds me close. The relief I was available is palpable.

He whispers near my ear. "You are my life. I'm grateful to you for being here."

"No place I would rather be except beside you. Mama never let me down. I won't do it to her. Our start may have been rocky, but she never wavered in support of our relationship. Not once in twenty years did I wonder if I was enough for you in her eyes. We're a team."

"You kind of like me, huh?"

I smile against the crook of his neck and reply, "I love you from the depths of my soul."

He pulls back. "How am I supposed to follow that?"

"There isn't a wrong reply."

His brain turns for a long moment. I wonder what he's thinking. As long as his thoughts involve us for the rest of our lives, I'm on board.

"Meeting you on a random rooftop in New York City was the best thing that has ever happened to me."

"More than winning the Super Bowl?"

"Without question." He kisses the tip of my nose and settles onto the couch beside Mama.

Tonight, she and her sons agreed not to make any rash decisions about her living situation. Mama admits two falls is a concern overall and is willing to have someone check on her more frequently. Progress, in my opinion.

CHAPTER TWENTY-EIGHT

KELLAN

This season has been heavy on highs, but the low cuts deep. Last week, the trifecta was one win away from a berth in the Super Bowl. During the third quarter of the conference final, Jordan suffered a gruesome leg injury. The television crew didn't replay it, not even once. Seeing him writhing in pain after the whistle blew nearly had me hurling on the sideline. The team made a circle around him and the training staff. Then we waited with bated breath for Jordan to indicate his status. Eventually, he gave a thumbs-up.

My stomach twisted when he called me and Press closer before they drove him off the field.

"I need you to carry the ball home today and through the big game," Jordan stated and curled his fist.

Preston and I created a triangle and promised to secure another ring. Should we have? Probably not. Did we mean it? Absolutely. We buckled down for the remainder of the game and eked out a three-point win.

In the locker room, Preston pulls me aside. "Can you meet me for film and planning tomorrow after training?"

We have made a preliminary plan for both potential opponents already. However, Jordan was included in those plays.

"Yeah. We need to revamp half of our playbook." Devastation is evident in his tone. Both Press and I pushed Jordan to choose this team. "You know better than to blame yourself."

Preston nods, and we bro hug and leave the facility. When I slide into the driver's seat, I wake my phone. It was silent during today's session.

Dolce: Reach out when you are finished for the day.

Instead of checking the rest of my messages, I call my girl.

"How are you?" she asks immediately. No small talk, just understanding of how crappy my day was.

"I'm dealing. Jordan had surgery, and we had a video call. He asked if we would give him space."

"That sucks."

It's the last thing I want to do. My gut tells me to crash his hospital room and take care of the kids for a bit. I won't, though I feel as if I should. "It does, but I will honor his requests." I can see her furrowed brows in my mind.

"Requests, plural?"

Damn! "Yeah, he asked Preston and I to earn another ring for the trifecta before he was carted off. I didn't mention it when we talked after the game. I'm sorry."

"No apology necessary. I asked Ellis to make changes to the schedule. Hell, I gave him a heads-up months ago."

"You knew then?"

She laughs. The sound hits me center mass. It always has from the moment we met. Her melodic chuckles always soothe me even from afar. “I was being proactive. Was I sure? Of course not. I had hope though.”

“My biggest fan.”

She laughs again. “I think Mama might give me a run for my money.”

“Fair enough. I’ll call you tonight. I hope your scenes are less than four takes for the next week.”

“Best ever! Love you.”

I reply in kind and end the call. A huge meal and falling into bed is in my future. After parking in the garage, I start some laundry and preheat the oven. Carol’s contact information was included in one of the envelopes in Demi’s gift box to me while she’s filming. In addition to watching over the Malibu property, she prepares and ships meals to me. Especially now during the playoffs, I appreciate the ease and lack of work on my part to eat well.

My phone vibrates on the island.

Dolce: Ellis approved my changes with a seat in our box.

Me: Hell yes! Talk more later. Love you.

Dolce: Love you.

Containing my joy is impossible. While Demi was present the last instance I won the Super Bowl, we didn’t experience it together. This time not only will she be there but my entire family as well.

I'm excited to see Mama again in person. We didn't visit for the holiday season this year. The logistics simply didn't pan out. We were able to hang out over a video call for a short time on the day though. The family is traveling the day before the game and staying at the Malibu property. Carol and I have been in contact, and she is prepared for a full house. I also requested security for Demi and my family on the sideline and in the stadium. I refuse to take any chances, especially after her Oscar win has garnered additional attention for her.

Demi stayed with Mama after her second fall instead of at my home for the duration of filming. There was some reluctance on Mama's part, but overall, the situation worked out. When Demi returned to Arizona, we set up a companion for Mama. Violet, a lovely young woman, visits her at least four days a week. Her duties include keeping Mama company and light housework. My siblings and I would've preferred to handle caring for Mama ourselves. Reality is cruel. None of us has enough time due to work, distance between our homes, and family commitments.

My personal guilt for leaving DC returned with a vengeance on the flight to see her. Grateful doesn't begin to describe how I feel about Demi agreeing to relocate. From the stories she shared, her and Mama had a great time catching up. Mama shared a few family recipes during their stint as roommates. Admittedly, Demi failed when she tried to prepare the prized blueberry pie. The effort counts in my book. The dessert didn't look good, but it was delicious.

I refocus on Coach at the front of the room. We're in squad meetings today before the final round of interviews. I'm anxious for it to be over. The faster today passes, the sooner I can hold Demi before the Super Bowl. Knowing she was there to support me the first time means more than I can express. Despite our relationship status, her presence on the biggest day of my career to date back then makes me happy. Elated barely covers my emotions for this chance at a second coveted championship ring.

Media commitments pass quickly, and I make it to the team hotel and lock myself in my room. I considered driving to the Malibu house, but with traffic, it won't yield enough time to visit before I need to turn around for curfew. I hear you, grown men with a curfew. It's more of a guideline, but keeping my mind and body right to win is a priority.

Dolce: I'm home with the fam. Want a video call?"

Me: Hell yes!

My family takes turns sitting at the island where Demi set up her laptop.

"Uncle Kellan, are you going to win?" my ten-year-old nephew, Josiah, inquires.

Yes. I don't share my innermost thoughts with him. "My team and I are prepared as best we can be. The goal is victory. Are you excited to be at the game?"

He nods enthusiastically and runs away.

I laugh and then my niece Maddie pops into view. "Good luck tomorrow."

"Thanks, Mads. What are you looking forward to?"

"The celebrity watching," she replies without a second thought.

I raise an eyebrow. Overall, she has been chill about Demi. There will be other stars in the box and nearby. I'm not offended exactly. It makes sense. She's a teenager whose uncle is an NFL star and future aunt is an Oscar-winning actress. I didn't propose… yet.

She clears her throat and adds, "A win for your team, of course."

The rest of my family offers quick well-wishes. Then Mama takes a seat.

"You have worked so hard to get here. Jordan will be rooting you on from afar."

Leave it to her to bring every doubt to the surface with one sentence. "Thanks. How are you?"

"Excellent. Violet is a wonderful help at home. Demi has been doting on me since she arrived."

"Good. Your comfort with having a helper saves me the trouble of asking you to move into the casita permanently."

Mama smiles. "I won't intrude on your relationship or my other children. Good luck tomorrow. Remember to have fun above all else."

She always added those words since I was a kid. "Love you, Mama."

Demi's voice comes through the phone. "Hey, give me a second. I'm moving into the bedroom."

After a few abrupt shifts and flips on the screen, my gorgeous woman appears. I was skeptical we could pull off a relationship with our demanding careers. The understatement of the year, in my opinion. I've loved Demi since the moment I laid eyes on her. Our roller-coaster ride proves love isn't enough. Maintaining a relationship with your person takes planning, sacrifice, diligence, and patience. Finally, we figured that out this time around. When the clock expires at the end of this game, I intend to have two championship rings and ask for Demi to be mine forever.

Demi's voice drags me out of my thoughts. "How are you feeling? Physically, I mean."

Football is demanding and hard on the body. She's fully aware of the bruises, welts, and contusions I have each week despite the distance between us. "I'm good." A wave of sadness hits when I recall Jordan isn't. I shake away the thought. Injuries are part of the game. Press and I have to secure a victory for our hurt teammate… and ourselves as well. Our season has proven the front office was savvy in bringing the trifecta back together with a strong offensive line. Nothing short of a victory is acceptable.

"Kellan." Her tone indicates disbelief.

"Dolce." I stare into her cobalt eyes. "I'm good, physically and mentally. Preston and I changed the plays up and presented it the OC." OC is short for offensive coordinator. "He's on board."

"Good luck. I'll meet you on the home team logo when the game ends. Love you, KO."

"I'll be there. Love you."

She blows me a kiss and ends the call. If tomorrow wasn't a huge game, we would stay up until the wee hours of the morning talking. However, solid rest is necessary.

Unable to help myself, I knock on the adjoining door. Preston doesn't answer. Rather than worry, I pull out the playbook and review it one last time before grabbing some sleep.

Keeping with my routine is key to earning a win. I follow it as best I can from a hearty meal to running the scripted series in my mind to maintaining focus on the task of the day. There's only one… a win.

First thing, I send my stats to Demi and join the team in the lobby.

Me: Going big. One hundred twenty yards and two scores. Love you.

Dolce: Hell yes! Go get 'em. Love you.

Hours have passed, the national anthem has been belted out by a newer country artist, and we lose the coin toss. Our opponent elects to defer until the second half. It's an interesting strategy. Either way, I tug on my helmet and line up. The roar of the crowd disappears when I focus only between the end lines. For the next sixty football minutes, my teammates and I are determined to accomplish one more win as a group.

Preston receives the snap and drops back. The first play is a handoff, and the running back muscles forward. He gains eight yards. The second play of the drive is a slant route for me while the backup wideout runs a go route.

The tight spiral is in the air. I leap, tuck it under my arm, and dash up field for forty yards. Without celebration, I return the ball to the ref and join the huddle.

"DC 42, Manning 8," Preston calls out the play.

He's aiming big. *Let's get it!*

The ball sails in the air toward me near the goal line. I stretch as far as I can and haul it down. Pushing to my feet in the end zone, I point to my heart and then toward the luxury suites. The camera operators are amazing. They are aware of Demi's presence, and this time she welcomes being filmed. Demi copies the move and blows me a kiss. I fist-bump Press and scamper off the field.

"Hell yeah!" he shouts as we make our way to the bench.

I exude calm and urge him to sit beside me and the wideouts. The OC joins us, and we study the drive on the tablet. My priority is managing the biggest game of the season with the same diligence as the ones before. The work earned us this berth.

My teammates on the sideline shift together and bunch to the right. Our cornerback intercepts a pass and runs it back for another touchdown. We are seven minutes into this game and up by two scores.

Preston offers a fist bump, and we continue reviewing the offense.

Our defense stands up the opposing team at their twenty with ten-and-a-half minutes remaining in the second quarter.

In the huddle, Jordan's replacement, Bryce Hillman, rallies the group. "A long drive and a score. Get it!"

We clap and line up. The fullback breaks through the line and rushes forward, gaining fourteen yards. With a new set of downs, we fail to grab anything on first. Preston calls the same play from earlier. Works like a charm again. Preston rushes toward me, we chest bump, then I motion to Demi. Her gorgeous face is splashed on the big screen again. During my first Super Bowl game, she made a point not to be seen. Her request back then was to protect my heart and hers. Today we're willing to shout from the rafters of this stadium our commitment to each other.

Thirty minutes of play have expired, and we have a three-score lead as we scamper into the locker room.

This break will be longer due to the halftime show featuring a trio of R&B artists. While rare, I check my messages while I take a breather.

Jordan: I hope you see this. The safety can't handle you. Line up there. Tell Press.

Jordan: Overload the weak side and you will have a clear line to the end zone.

Jordan: YES!!!

I smile, knowing he's watching and we're doing right by him.

Me: Thanks, bro.

Jordan: You need one more to break the record. Get it!

Me: I'll do my best.

In the back of my mind, I knew earning a place in the record books was feasible, but chasing records isn't my reason for playing the game I love. Much like Demi and earning Oscars and other awards, I suit up because it's my passion and I excel between the hash marks, not for accolades. I would be lying if I didn't acknowledge the slight desire to earn this one. Playing in the big game once and winning is a dream. Multiple opportunities are rare air. Arguments can be made on either side whether I belong in the conversation of tight ends in the upper echelon of this league.

Preston plops down in the seat beside me. "Wanna get another score?"

In a rare moment of ego, I reply, "Yes."

For the remaining minutes of halftime, my QB1 lays out a plan to win the game and solidify my position atop a list or two in the record books.

Our opponent stifles us offensively for the third quarter. Luckily, our line stops them as well.

In the huddle as we take the field, Press says, "They can't hold us scoreless for another quarter. Peyton 3, Dash 20."

This play is for me to run a go route along the end line.

I catch his gaze and acknowledge him.

The pass sails through the air and falls into my arms for a massive fifty-yard gain.

Preston runs to me, and we jump together in celebration. If the other team realizes our plan or they don't want me to beat them again, I expect double coverage.

Press passes to Hillman and adds a few runs into the mix. Patience is one of his strongest qualities.

Our OC calls a play where we have four receivers. It will force our opponent into single-man coverage.

I signal Press, and he calls an audible. A crossing slant which leads me into the end zone and a record-breaking touchdown. I secure the ball until

I hand it off to the sideline for safekeeping and motion my heart in the stands. My entire family is cheering in the box as well as Val and Finn. My third score today puts us up by twenty points as the clock dwindles.

Our defense holds the opponent to a three and out. They failed to gain ten yards and punt the ball to the opponent.

With less than two minutes left in the game, we recover an on-side kick. Then we take a knee rather than run more plays.

Each second the clock ticks, my chest expands with pride. We did it!

The clock expires, and confetti rains down on the turf.

As soon as I'm able, I run toward our spot. Demi leaps into my arms. I didn't think twice and neither did she.

As I spin with her in my arms, she shouts, "I'm so proud of you!"

"Thanks."

"A new title too," she adds.

I see this as the perfect time. "What do you say to another for both of us?"

She adds space to stare into my eyes.

I bring my mouth near her ear. "Be my wife."

"Yes!" she shouts. My proposal in the midst of my family, friends, and national television was private enough. No one has a clue other than Demi and me. I kiss her deeply and set her on the colorful turf.

We celebrate our victory with our friends and family and share our personal news. Once we arrive home, we revel in our two wins tonight… a championship ring for me and golden bands for both of us.

Thank you so much for reading *Our Touchdown Script.*

Ready for a new Soren HEA? Which sister will fall next?

Did you love *Our Touchdown Script?*

Thank you for taking the time to read it. I hope you loved it!
If you liked this book or another one of my books, please consider posting a review.
A short line or two will be perfect! It helps indie authors like me get noticed. I appreciate your support and feedback.

COMING SOON

Two new stories are coming soon!

A Soren Novel

A Blackthorne Novel

MY BOOKS

YORK BEACH SERIES

A New Beginning with You

Taking A Chance on Me

Just One More

Kiss You Like You're Mine

Only with Him

My Once in a Lifetime

THE CAPPELLI FAMILY

Chasing Forever

Chasing My Sunshine

Worth the Chase

Chasing After You

Chasing Someday

MORGAN BROTHERS SERIES

One Unforgettable Favor

Until I Kissed You

Always Have, Always Will

BLACKTHORNE SECURITY

Protecting My Forever

Protecting Our Future

Protecting Us

Hers to Protect

Protecting our Family

Protecting Home

MATCHMAKERS' BOOK CLUB

For Love & Coffee

For Love & Basketball

For Love & Cookies

For Love & Photos

SCALA TALENT & SPORTS MANAGEMENT

Moonshot

Our Messy Sequel

THE SOREN FAMILY

Unexpected Forever

Unexpected Serendipity

All my books in one place: www.nicolevidal.com/books

www.ingramcontent.com/pod-product-compliance
Lightning Source LLC
LaVergne TN
LVHW010647110826
845149LV00014B/2978

* 9 7 8 1 9 6 1 3 6 5 7 3 5 *